Metaphorosis

October 2022

Beautifully made speculative fiction

Also from Metaphorosis

<u>Metaphorosis Magazine</u>

Metaphorosis: Best of 20xx
Metaphorosis 20xx: The Complete Stories
annual issues, from 2016

Monthly issues

<u>Plant Based Press</u>

Best Vegan Science Fiction & Fantasy
annual issues, 2016-2020

from B. Morris Allen:
Chambers of the Heart: speculative stories
Susurrus
Allenthology: Volume I
Tocsin: and other stories
Start with Stones: collected stories
Metaphorosis: a collection of stories

<u>Verdage</u>

Reading 5X5 x3: Changes
Reading 5X5 x2: Duets
Score – an SFF symphony
Reading 5X5: Readers' Edition
Reading 5X5: Writers' Edition

<u>Vestige</u>

The Nocturnals, by Mariah Montoya

Metaphorosis

October 2022

edited by
B. Morris Allen

ISSN: 2573-136X (online)
ISBN: 978-1-64076-238-1 (e-book)
ISBN: 978-1-64076-239-8 (paperback)

Metaphorosis
a magazine of speculative fiction

from
Metaphorosis Publishing

Neskowin

October 2022

Problems of the Flesh

Hamilton Perez

It was the month of the apocalypse, and I'd come home to a house of shadows and gloom. The curtains and blinds were all shut, barring any light except what leaked through the door. The air smelled like spoiled fast food. No sound came from within—not his labored breath from the recliner, not even his favorite sitcom laughing hysterically at itself.

That was the first time I doubted.

Not that there hadn't been moments before then. Moments that didn't feel right, I guess, despite having every assurance they would be—*they were*—from the one person who really could say definitively. But it was coming home to darkness that made me wonder if things weren't as they should be. Weren't as promised.

"My Lord ...?" I called, but I was met with the same silence, the same dark. *That's fine*, I assured myself, arms shaking, chest tight. *Everything's fine ...* "Lord Grivvux?" I tried again, my voice thin as prayer.

Something crashed across the living room floor, and *"Dammit! Is that you?"* his voice called from the black.

Only then did I remember to breathe, though it came out in ragged, uncertain laughter.

The Supreme Lord—Maker, Keeper, Destroyer of Worlds—was alright.

"Yes, my Lord!" I said, fumbling with the bags and keys as I stepped inside, grinning with dumb relief. "It is I, your faithful servant—"

"Sam, please," the Lord God cut me off. "You really don't need to go on like that. Once you've helped your god in and out of the tub, I'd say you're on a more familiar basis." The recliner groaned as he rose to meet me.

"Ah! Yes! Of course!" I said awkwardly, kicking the door shut behind me. "Forgive me, King of Kings, Lord Grivvux of the Permafire."

"It's fine, Sam … And again, *Grux* will be fine."

"*Grux* …" I said, trying on the word, but it still didn't feel right. Thousands of years ago, it was Grivvux—not *Grux*—who was worshiped all across Sumer. The fatted calf was venerated and slain at the Altar of Grivvux, not *Grux*. When our priests and acolytes were seduced by other gods, the family order kept faith with Grivvux, not *Grux*. "I, uh, like it."

I shuffled past him, trying not to catch the sour smell of his skin. No matter how hard I scrubbed, he always smelled like unwashed feet. It was just one more thing to deal with since his long-prophesied return. There was no telling the cause of it all—if it was disbelief in the old powers, the unchecked metastasis of sin, or global warming—but the Lord God had taken human form and now he was, well, *too* human, I guess …

"They had fresh lamb today!" I called over my shoulder.

"How fresh?" he asked, following behind me, his rough soles scratching the hardwood.

"Well, it's not still kicking …"

"Ah ..."

Was that disappointment? I wondered, making my way to the kitchen blindly and reaching for the light.

"Please don't—"

The world flashed before I heard him. The Lord God shielded himself with his arm, revealing skin littered with sores. I killed the light, and then we just stood there, embarrassed in the dark.

"Is that because of me?" I finally asked.

"It's best you try not to think about it," he said, but I was already tallying up the day's sins. *I flipped off the Mercedes that cut me off. I lied to the beggar asking for change. I snagged the last box of fiber supplements from an old woman.*

"Did you get the ceremonial robes?" he asked.

"Um, yes, *well* ..." I began sorting through plastic bags, searching by feel. "Linnamin's was having a sale." I withdrew two neatly-folded robes. They were black, but presently so was everything.

"It doesn't matter where they came from, Sam." The Lord God walked across the kitchen and turned on the patio light, letting in just enough for us to see by. "So long as we take this seriously."

I looked doubtfully at the mass-produced bathrobes.

Lord Grivvux returned to examine one, brushing it softly with his rough hands. "These will do fine ..." he said, pressing the robe against his cheek as though some secret magic were sewn into its design, some hope only the righteous and wise could discern.

"They have a three hundred thread count ..." I said.

That night, we knelt before the fireplace in our ceremonial bathrobes, the fire eating the logs with a crackle and spark that sounded like laughter.

"What's this supposed to do again?" I asked, uncertainly.

"It's a minor restoration spell, Sam. Nothing to be apprehensive about. We're simply appealing to the powers beyond to grant me a greater form, one that isn't in need of such maintenance. One that might inspire a bit more *awe* ..."

"Oh."

Lord Grivvux sensed my doubt and clarified, "So I can better guard against the Last End, Sam."

"Yes, of course. The Big Wet One."

"What?"

"Oh, sorry, nothing. That's just what Mom used to call the Final Flood. Sort of a joke, really. I guess that's not appropriate anymore ..."

He said nothing and continued the preparations.

It was Mom who first taught me the old faith: the rituals, spells, and prophecies. She was pretty transparent about it being what soured her marriage, why Dad ran off before I was born. *It's okay, Samuel,* she'd told me, *Lord Grivvux of the Permafire is your* true *Father, as he is for all.* She always believed the Lord had big plans for me, but I doubt even she dreamed I'd be the Chosen One to herald our Lord before the end.

Granted, it's not like there were a lot of runners-up.

After Mom passed, I became the last of our order—a lonely ember cooling in the ash. The Grivvuxian Acolytes once comprised thousands, but believers dropped off every year the Lord did not return. You could hardly blame them. Some had witnessed the rise of new gods and queer religions, each promising the same things: peace, prosperity, the end of the world.

Me, I waited forty-three years for the one true God to return—to realize my purpose, or learn if I even had one. So I did what most people do while they wait for things to happen.

I got a job. I paid my bills. I did my time.

It was the planetary alignment that changed all that. Before then, the signs were already rolling in, but I was too blind or stubborn to see them. Toads croaked outside my window—*GRIVV-ux ... GRIVV-ux ...* The words *He doth come* appeared while making dinner, materializing out of noodles, eggs, or ground beef.

But the planets aligning was the promised sign—they told me when Lord Grivvux was coming, and where he would be. I didn't even know it was happening until an overzealous intern cornered me in the breakroom with it, hoping to initiate some early networking through what was surely to him just an interesting fact.

"Pretty neat, huh? I'm Jimmy—Jim—James!" he stammered nervously before thrusting forth a rigid hand.

"I have to go!" I dropped my coffee and ran to check if what he told me was true, and sure enough, the end was nigh.

That was the last time I stepped foot in that office. An eighteen-year corporate climb abandoned for a higher purpose. *For the greater good.* And for all I know my coffee is still puddled on the breakroom floor and *Jimmy-Jim-James* is running the place.

Things didn't turn out quite like I imagined, though.

"It is ready," said the Lord God solemnly. "First, the mustard seeds, for they contain the Kingdoms of Heaven."

Amongst the assorted ingredients, I found a small pouch. I poured the seeds into my palm and cast them into the fire. The flames took the seeds ungratefully, nipping at my hand.

"Next, Wolf's Claw."

I fumbled through bundles of herbs.

"It's the green one ... white hairs ..."

I found the spindly plant and threw it in. A white light flashed, revealing shadowy figures standing all around us, and when the light dissolved, they too were gone.

"Who were they?" I asked.

"The Watchers. Do not fret. Their presence is a good omen. Now the pennyroyal. Purple."

I had questions. I always had questions. I wasn't *supposed* to have questions though, so I kept my mouth shut, and withdrew a long string of purple bulbs and threw it over the blaze. The fire turned a lavender shade and burned so hot that sweat ran down my forehead and cheeks.

"Now for the mandrake, the one that looks like a—"

"Yeah, I'm familiar with this guy." I took the vaguely human-shaped root from the pile of spell components.

Lord Grivvux watched me, dumbfounded. "*You* know the mandrake?"

"Sort of. Just from Harry Potter." The root roused to life in my hand, gently unfurling its limbs like I'd woken it from a long, restful sleep.

Lord Grivvux narrowed his eyes, considering. "Harry Potter ... Is this some sorcerer that you know?"

"Ah, well, he's a wizard actually, but he's not really—"

Amazement washed over my God's face, a confluence of excitement and frustration, and I felt deeply that I'd done something wrong. "Sam, I wish you had spoken sooner! We should absolutely consult with this wizard before performing the ritual! This could be the break we've been waiting for!"

"No, no, he's like, a character," I fumbled. "In a story. Books. Movies. He isn't real ..."

"Oh," said the Lord God, blank-faced.

"Yeah ..."

The mandrake twisted and writhed in my hand.

"Well ..." said the King of Kings.

"Should we not—"

"Please, proceed," he said with a passive gesture.

A crease opened along the mandrake's head, wailing pitifully, *"Noooo ..."*

"Yikes!" I startled. "Is it speaking?"

"Begging," said Lord Grivvux simply, as if this were expected. A mere fact of the world. I thought he might still be bugged about Harry Potter.

"Why now?" I asked.

"Being eaten or burned or thrown away, it can handle. But to be sacrificed, to be turned over to the Darkness, that is another matter entirely."

"Oh."

"Indeed."

I went to toss it on the fire, but Lord Grivvux stopped me.

"No," he said. "The mandrake is blameless, completely without sin. It must choose to enter the flames. Otherwise the Watchers may not accept our offering."

A hundred questions rattled through my mind. Who were these *Watchers*? They couldn't be gods in their own right, for there was only one God, and Grivvux—not *Grux*—was his name. So what did it mean that they could refuse him? Did freewill really extend that far? I couldn't tell if that made my Lord more godly or less, but just then the fire's warmth began to wane. We were running out of time.

"Does it need convincing?" I asked, preparing my best speech about the salvation of many and the greater good.

"Not from you." Lord Grivvux took the mandrake and cradled it in his arms, whispering to it in some language I could not understand—some language soft and beautiful and profound.

Like a tamed infant, the mandrake grew calm. The Lord set it gently onto the hardwood floor, and with quiet dignity, the noble root stood up and marched steadfast into the fire. Fingers of violet flame wrapped around it, guiding it in until it was swallowed by light. My Lord God smiled, all worry wiped from his face. But behind the wisps of flame, shadows swung against smoke and stone. Somewhere in the fire, life crumbled woefully to ash.

Lord Grivvux leaned forward, closed his eyes, and blew out the fire like it was only a birthday candle. Maybe it was, I thought.

In the smoldering ash, small specks now glistened and shone.

"Draw forth a mustard seed," my Lord commanded.

I found a tiny kernel, bright as a star, and pinched it between my fingers.

"Here! Here!" said my Lord anxiously. I dropped the seed in the center of his palm, and he blew on it delicately, causing it to roll about, growing like a snowball until the mustard seed filled his palm. "Yes ... *yes* ..." said the Lord God as thin green shoots twisted out, branching into alien tendrils. "Come to me ..." Once they touched his cheek, they cast a brilliant light through his skin, until golden rays seeped from his every pore.

It's working ... I thought, amazed.

The image reminded me of when Mom would take me camping, how at the end of every ghost story, she'd put the flashlight in her mouth so her cheeks glowed amber, pink, and gold. Now it made me laugh with melancholy joy—the kind of joy that's known loss yet also knows that no one is ever lost forever.

The light spread through my Lord's body, until he positively *glowed* from scalp to toe, and where the tendril rest, the worn skin cracked like it was only a shell, revealing a golden cheek, golden eye, and golden brow hidden just beneath the surface.

It's true, I thought. *It's all true. It's all real* ... And no words can capture the unutterable joy of that moment. The joy of knowing I'd invested my heart well, that I'd been on the right path all along. The joy as full and ineffable as he was.

But my God blinked, or I did.

The tendril faltered, turned black, wilted to the floor. My king diminished, returned to his tired, frail form.

"What happened?" I asked.

Grivvux sighed. "Magic is a living thing, Sam ... and it has too long been neglected in this world."

He rose, defeated.

I was about to ask what was next, but he simply dropped the ceremonial bathrobe to the floor, revealing his scarred and red-cratered body, and walked silently to his room.

"We'll find the answer, my king!" I shouted after him. "Whatever it takes!"

The only response was the sound of his door shutting me out.

When I'd first found God, hunched and frail in an abandoned church, I'd thought: *That's about right. Not what I expected at all. That's what you want in a god.* So I guess I was willing to overlook what he said when I approached:

"Please don't. Just stay back. It's all wrong. Just let me go ..."

Growing up in a religious household, you think the hardest part of faith is wondering if you're wrong. If in those moments of raw need and vulnerability you're just talking to the wind. And if He isn't real, what is? What virtues or beauty have any significance if not handed down from above? The most frightening thing you can imagine is not the seven hells or the final flood, it's a world without value. Then you meet God face to face and know —*really know*—that we're not alone.

There's someone out there. Someone listening. Someone giving purpose and meaning to all things.

You'd think it would be easier after that, but sometimes I missed the not knowing.

The morning after the ritual, I came home to find him on the back patio, talking to the birds. There were three of them: a blue jay, a robin, and a lowly pigeon, all perched side by side along the fence. They whistled and chirped, and Grivvux laughed and whistled back.

Soon more birds swooped in. A whole congregation. A murder—or is that only with crows? They lined the fence like springtime decorations. Their songs were no longer sweet melodies, but busy and discordant, too many voices speaking and disagreeing at once.

Then the lowly pigeon that was there all along stepped forward. It purred at Grivvux, who sighed and whistled back. I couldn't begin to guess what they were discussing, but at the end of it, the pigeon flew to his hand, nuzzling affectionately at his thumb and cooing a strange, sad sound. "Thank you, old friend," said Grivvux as he turned and brought the pigeon inside.

He nodded casually in my direction as he entered, and before I could ask how he was feeling, he tossed the pigeon down his throat like it was just a couple of aspirin. I sat there, mouth gaping, wide-eyed and dumb, while Grivvux leaned with one arm against the kitchen counter, gradually composing himself.

"They remember ..." he said at last, and turned to face me. "I think I feel better."

"Maybe that's the answer ..." I said. *"Birds!"*

Grivvux cringed and waved me off. "Sam, do you have any idea how many birds it would take to put me in just *fair* health?"

"It doesn't matter!" I protested. "Whatever it takes! It's for the greater good!"

"I appreciate your fervor. Did you get the pills?"

It was difficult taking a deity to the doctor. He didn't have a social security number, insurance, or credit cards. And he didn't get sick like people. He didn't get cancer or the flu. He got Despair and Disbelief, Exile and Oblivion. The silver lining is that those conditions have a lot of the same symptoms as the stuff people get, which is why I'd started bribing a pharmacist at the drugstore down the street.

"She wasn't working today," I said.

He nodded vaguely before gripping his stomach. "Maybe you should get her number," he said, bracing against the kitchen counter as a sudden wave of Dread doubled him over.

Generally speaking, bribes fall under the wide umbrella of sin. Granted, a lot of things do, but that doesn't warrant a hand wave, no matter who you are. Unless you're God, I guess, and you're really that desperate, and something really has to be done.

I mean, if the Lord gives his blessing, how can it be a sin?

I still don't know.

Early in his convalescence, Grivvux went into an all-night trance to find someone that could help us. I was never too keen on that idea. Wasn't I supposed to be the one to help? Wasn't that why I'd kept my whole life on hold, and then abandoned all I'd worked for once he finally showed? But when God says *Go for help*, you do not say, *My Lord, I'm right here!*

Her name was Arielle. She was working two jobs to afford the medical bills brought on by her husband's sudden diagnosis of stage-4 leukemia. I knew this before she told me, of course. Grivvux had searched for someone in need, someone desperate enough to help other desperate people. I suppose we were lucky that she happened to be a pharmacist.

Over the months, a sort of quiet camaraderie had developed between us. We were both trapped in our situations, unsure how to move forward, doing whatever we could to keep afloat. Sometimes I wondered if she dreamed what I dreamed—just running away, escaping the chains of duty, the chains of being chosen.

"How's he doing today?" she asked the morning after he ate a bird.

"Getting better some," I said, wondering if we'd have to find an ornithologist struggling to make ends meet. "It's hard to say, though ..."

"Ah, I'm sorry, hon. I know how it is." She rubbed at her ring like a nervous tic.

"How are you holding up?" I asked.

"Ah ..." she said wistfully, lost in thought. "When I left this morning he was feeling better. Watching TV on the couch, splayed out in his boxers and ratty t-shirt. *Barbarian.* It felt oddly normal, though. So I guess I'm good."

"Thank God for good days."

She laughed, dryly. "Not sure I'd thank God if I met him, but to each their own."

The hidden truth of this struck like a spear in my side. Made me wonder if there wasn't something we could do to help, if the Lord could heal her husband, or restore their finances with his weight in gold. But without their plight, Arielle would have no need to help us, and then where would the world be?

Suddenly uncomfortable, I cleared my throat and offered the typical folded papers. Arielle looked at them and frowned. She glanced over her shoulder once, then withdrew a bag from under the counter and passed it to me. I thanked her and turned to leave when I remembered my Lord's firm command.

Maybe you should get her number.

"Listen," I said, turning back. "I was thinking maybe it would be a good idea to exchange phone numbers."

Her brow raised skeptically.

"I just mean—no, I was, uh, thinking, that is, given what we're each going through, I don't know. If you ever want to talk with someone that understands ..."

I arrived home still rubbing the waxy receipt paper between my fingers, unsure how I felt about it—how I *should* feel about it. I was nervous and excited and enticed and I was ashamed for feeling nervous and excited and enticed.

I periodically opened the folded note to gaze at the numbers.

Grivvux was in the backyard again, this time gardening in a blue-and-white Hawaiian shirt and brown pants, both covered in smears of dark soil. On his head was a beach hat with a sunflower design. He'd been tending Mom's garden, which had turned pitiful and weed-grown from neglect ever since her death.

He startled to find me watching him. "Sam! I'm glad you're here," he said, composing himself. "I have a new spell for us to try." He turned back to his work and thrust a spade into the soil, withdrawing a dark pile of earth. "I'm feeling very optimistic," he said, and I could hear the smile in his voice.

"I got her number," I said, feeling a strange tug at my cheeks.

Grivvux stopped digging.

"For your pills," I clarified.

"Yes … But not just."

My cheeks warmed. "She's married," I said, a little too quickly.

He poked at the soil ponderously before looking over his shoulder. "There are hard times ahead, Sam. Much will be demanded in order to bring about this world's salvation." He returned to the dirt, delicately placing a pink amaryllis. "Do not spurn what joy has offered. You both should take what solace you can while it's available."

"I don't know, my Lor—*Grux*. Her husband is *dying* …"

"I know." Grux brushed the flower's petals, and then turned to face me. "Sam, this world is naught but shadows and wind. A passing thing, an illusion. All that matters—*really matters*—are the lives caught in it, the lives I intend to save. The only groom is I, and the world is my bride. Call her."

He glanced past me. "Oh hello there, Penny!" He walked over to talk to the neighbor on the other side of the fence. "I'm feeling much better today, thank you. I see your petunias are coming in beautifully. Did you use the coffee grounds like I suggested?"

I met with Arielle the following Wednesday. Not exactly date night, which was fine because it wasn't exactly a date. It was just coffee with a friend. Not even a friend really, an acquaintance—an accomplice. But an hour before meeting, she texted to see if we could get drinks at a local bar instead. And she pushed us from a casual four o'clock to half past eight.

The Mariana was all in a nautical theme, with crossed oars and thick, knotted ropes hanging from the walls. Appropriate, I thought, for the end of the world, the flood that would wash away our cities, our cultures, our sins.

Above the entryway hung a rowboat, old and well-used, with chipped paint and warped wood, darkened so that it almost looked wet with sea spray. It was hard not to stare at it, to imagine it undulating gently over the Pacific, with no one to answer to and nothing to be ashamed of, just rowing, rowing, forever …

"Sam?"

I turned absently when her hand brushed my arm and I jumped in surprise, almost spilling the iced water I'd ordered to occupy my hands.

"Oh hey, Arielle!" I blurted uncomfortably, feeling that vast ocean evaporate around me.

She just laughed.

"So, this is going out …" she said with a wry smile, glancing about the bar.

"Yeah," I nodded. "I guess this is something people do now. We'll see if it takes off."

We ordered drinks and clinked our glasses a bit too hard, the sound reverberating like something delicate warning it might break, but we just laughed and sipped.

The conversation was stilted at first, struggling to navigate the standard *get-to-know-you's* when we already knew so much about each other, but only our sad and intimates. Fortunately, Arielle was intent on avoiding these subjects, dismissing her own with a flippant, "We can skip that, we both know everything's fucked." She punctuated it with a boisterous, if nihilistic, laugh.

Instead, we focused on the relief of going out again, and looking back wistfully to the warmth of summers past. Under the counter, our knees brushed occasionally, stirring awkward laughter and fumbled apologies.

Arielle told me how she missed kayaking, missed floating down the American River on hot days with a cooler full of PBR. She missed the sun hanging like a jewel over the water, and the river-smell on her skin when she headed back home.

"I'd be tipsy as hell by the time we reached shore," she said, "so my husband would have to drive home while I napped in the back seat."

She began to laugh but stopped abruptly, seeming on the verge of tears before quietly composing herself, while the mere mention of her husband drew my chest tight, set my heart thundering against my ribs.

Arielle gave me a quizzical look, then appeared to recognize my discomfort. "Don't worry," she said casually, "he knows I'm here. We tell each other everything. Our marriage is like a church, we're open to everybody."

"Oh," I said, trying to conceal my surprise. "Oh," I said again. The faith was pretty old-school in how it defined marriage—and even more so in how it defined infidelity—but then in the 90's there were attempts to modernize, in the vain hope of drawing new believers. Would open marriages not fold into that? Wasn't love *love*, after all? I wondered if Grux knew, if that's why he said the only groom was him. Did that make this a real date? Did that make this okay? Who determines these things?

"What about you?" she asked.

"Me?"

"Yeah, have you always been taking care of your dad or was there some blessed before time you look back to when you wake in a cold sweat in the middle of the night and can't get back to sleep?" She laughed once in playful self-acknowledgment.

I opened my mouth to speak and realized that I had nothing to say. My childhood wasn't full of adventure or play, it was full of prophecy and tales of annihilation. Each day had opened and closed with prayer, and each prayer opened and closed with the pact:

The world forgets You, but we are not the world.

We hold no grand ambitions, no fanciful dreams of conceit.

We live but to die, born to usher in the end.

I was raised to shun the world; I didn't get to float downstream, and even after Mom passed, it never occurred to me that I could.

"Oh, I've always taken care of him," I said, taking a long sip, swallowing it down.

Arielle nodded. "See, I knew you were one of the good ones," she said with a wink, and finished her own beverage.

I blushed, and she teased me for blushing, and I blushed even more, and she laughed all the harder.

We ordered another round, and the night grew late in an instant. We were so engrossed in laughter and conversation that the owners had to come out and ask us to leave. Their employees had already cleared the tables and mopped around us. We snapped from our daze, apologized, tipped generously, apologized again, and headed out. "Sorry!" Arielle shouted back once they locked the doors behind us, and then we stumbled off together.

The night was crisp and cool and occasionally Arielle would lean against me as we walked off our buzz along the quiet midtown streets.

"… Where'd you park?" I asked lamely.

"Oh, I had an Uber drop me off," she said, pulling out her phone and opening the app.

"Arielle, I—"

"Please," she said, "everyone just calls me Ellie."

Ellie … I thought. *Of course!* Arielle didn't exactly roll off the tongue, but *Ellie* was laid back. *Ellie* was carefree. *Ellie* was inviting and warm.

"I could drive you home, if you like …"

The smile she gave me could melt the icecaps entire, and flood the earth in a rush of warm spray.

We lingered awhile in the driveway, heads down, eyes fixed on our own laps. Ellie's right hand turned the ring on her left, the diamond going over and under. Like a karmic wheel, I thought, turning endlessly, going nowhere. I wondered if it was a sign of second thoughts, or a prelude to something else.

"Thank you for this," she said, smiling. "I had a really good time tonight. It feels like it's been so long since I've gotten to do ... *anything.*"

Her smile cracked, then shattered, her face scrunching up, tears streaming. "I'm sorry!" She wiped desperately at her eyes, trying to dam the flood. "This has nothing to do with you," she said with a reassuring hand.

I felt tremendous guilt then. Would she even be in this situation if Grivvux hadn't come down? Would it be such a sin to wish he'd stayed up in his ethereal realm? Just let the world keep spinning with its small joys and heavy sins? I knew already the answer, of course, even if I tried to not know it.

"I know ..." I said, wiping my own cheek.

Her hand reached for mine, and I could feel the wet spots of tears on her skin. Our eyes met, vulnerable and aching. It felt like a call. I shifted closer, but she dropped her head and looked away.

Silence filled the car as our walls resurfaced. I withdrew back to my seat.

"Ughhh ..." she groaned, then laughed and wiped the last tears from her eyes. "What are we doing?" she asked, more to herself than to me it seemed.

"Just what we've been doing," I said, more thinking aloud than answering her. "Trying to stay afloat."

When she kissed me, it was as unexpected as the rapture. Her lips tasted like honey and milk and the dreams you thought could never come true. She pressed against me, her fingers sliding through my hair, pulling me closer until it hurt, blissfully.

I came home, body tingling, lips raw and electric. The house was dark and I didn't even mind. "Hello!" I called, but there was no answer. "Grux?" The house remained quiet. A thought pierced me: *What if I killed him with my sins?* I checked in the kitchen, the patio, turning on lights everywhere as I went, but illuminating nothing.

Had the Lord God died in my care? Had I failed him, failed every living soul on the planet? Were we doomed because of me? Because I wasn't prepared enough for his return? Because I wasn't holy enough to make him whole?

Grux said it was okay, didn't he? Was he wrong about that? Can he be wrong? Is that even possible?

I went down the hall to the master bedroom that once belonged to my mother, and then to me, and now belonged to the Lord Supreme. The door was shut. *He probably just went to bed early*, I told myself. But then I heard his voice, faint but animated, on the other side. I pressed my ear to the door, straining to make out what was said: vague promises, pleas, weeping. *He's praying,* I realized. Listening closer, I caught the words, "Lord Grivvux of the Permafire."

He's praying to himself…

Embarrassed, I stepped away, but just then a loud bell chimed from my pocket and the voice beyond went quiet. I shook with shame and cleared my throat. "My lord, I'm, uh, home. *Grux*, I mean … Hi …"

"Hello, Sam," the voice carried through the door. "I'd like to be alone tonight."

"Sure, I, um, things happened with Ellie."

"I know."

I gulped and retreated to my room. On my phone was an urgent bank notification about a suspicious purchase. I ran the numbers in my head—several rounds of drinks at a high end bar, tips.

I went to check the account, worrying over how much I'd spent. Sure, gold was something we could scrounge up, but it required Grux to do back-breaking labor and spirit-heavy spells, which was hard to justify so I could go on a date.

The flagged purchase was a mail order from *Etsy*. Rush delivery. A sacrificial blade crafted by "authentic virginized monks"—whatever those were. The blade itself was long and curved, with elaborate designs etched along the sides. It looked beautiful, but cruel.

I remembered that Grux had mentioned a new ritual, and ignored the warning.

As foreseen in the Grivvuxian prophecies of old, the weather on the last days of Earth was lovely. Maybe the prophets didn't phrase it quite like that—more like, "there will be no hint of cloud, let alone the harbingers of great rains that will wash away the cultures of man." But however you translate the old texts, those last days were indeed *blessed*.

Not that everyone could appreciate them.

A week after Ellie and I first went out, Grux still hadn't brought up the new spell or the sacrificial blade. He remained distant after Ellie and I started seeing each other, and as often as she came over, Grux still wouldn't let me introduce her.

"We'll meet," he told me. "Just not like that."

"You're no fun," I teased, and he said nothing in response for a long while, just watched me sprucing up the house, spraying air-freshener, hiding arcane instruments and ornaments that we'd experimented with to no avail.

"Be sure you don't grow too attached, Sam," he said warily. "We're here to save the world, not fall in love."

"I'm not in love," I said a bit too quickly. He looked at me, unconvinced. "I'm just doing what you told me," I said. "Like I always have. I'm taking joy while it's available. Isn't that what you said? This whole thing was your idea ... my Lord God."

"Yes, Sam. Of course. But remember that the key phrase there was *while it's available.* Sacrifices will have to be made, Sam. Some things can only be paid for in blood."

Immediately, the sacrificial blade from Etsy came to mind.

"I won't let any harm come to her," I said firmly. Ellie had paid enough. I wouldn't let her be dragged through more. This wasn't her faith, wasn't her fight, wasn't her price to pay.

Grux just looked confused, then nodded. "Yes," he said. "I understand. We'll discuss the end of the world at another time. Have fun on your date."

That night, when I brought Arielle home, we found roots of gold set on the kitchen counter like fresh pulled carrots. A folded note sat beside them with the address and rates of a nearby motel.

"What are those?" she asked, confused.

"Nothing," I said, quickly wrapping them in paper towels. "Dad likes to garden is all. He finds all sorts of weird things at the farmer's market!" I opened the fridge and tossed them in the crisper. They clanked metallically as vegetables seldom do.

Ellie didn't take well to the motel meetups. She didn't understand why we couldn't go back to my place anymore, or how I could afford a room every few nights.

"I just think it would be easier if we stayed at your place ..." she said.

"I know. But Dad doesn't like people coming over. It's much better this way."

"Maybe if you introduced us, he'd be okay with me." A mischievous grin took her face. "Or you could sneak me into your room like we're two stupid kids in high school."

"No," I told her. "I can't."

That gleeful expression dissolved into the familiar, everyday gloom. "Shouldn't you be with him, though?" she said, pulling away. It wasn't a question, and I knew we weren't talking about the Lord Supreme. It was him. *Her* him. "Doesn't he need you close by?"

Her eyes turned from me, scanning the room as if seeing it for the first time in all its drab lifelessness. There was no love or life in this room. Everything was sterile, but only superficially. Her eyes bloomed with wonder and disgust, and refused to meet mine.

"He's fine," I said, drawing her back. "If there's trouble, he'll call. Trust me." She was unconvinced, feeling further from me now than ever. If only I could tell her that the author of the universe had given his blessing. Or that the motel was his idea.

"There are hard times ahead," I found myself saying. "Don't spurn what joy has offered. We should take what joy we can while it's available."

Her eyes looked into mine, weighing the words uncertainly. "This isn't joy," she said, tossing her purse onto the pleather chair. "This is staying afloat." She sat on the foot of the bed, and began taking off her heels. "Well?" This while gesturing at my pants with a dismissive hand.

It all works out just fine. That's how the world ends, I told myself this as things fell apart, but there was no conviction in that old faith.

Ellie called me in tears while I waited at the motel. Said something had happened, she was on her way to the hospital. "It's over," she said. "I have to go. I'm sorry."

"I'm sorry too," I said, but she was already gone.

The house was dark when I came home. *Of course it's dark*, I thought. *Why would there be any light in the house of the lord?* I threw my jacket toward the ottoman, heard the buttons scrape the floor, and left it. "Grux?" I called, but there was no answer. Something turned in my stomach—a bad feeling. I wondered if Despair had finally caught up with him, if the pills had only put off the inevitable a few weeks. "My lord?"

Nothing.

I switched on the front lights, but the room stayed dark. In the kitchen, it was the same. The power must have gone out. But then I saw the streetlight over the back fence, its amber rays seeping into the kitchen.

And I saw *them.*

Dark figures stood outside, shadows looking in. *The Watchers.* Almost as soon as I spotted them, the streetlight flickered and died, the shadows melting into night. *Their presence is a good omen*, I remembered and tried not to be afraid.

Blindly, I made my way down the hall to the master bedroom. The door hung halfway open. "*Grux?*" I called in, leaning to peer inside. Enough moonlight came in from the open window that I could faintly make out the shape of the bed. Feathers blew across the floor in a haunting dance.

I was too afraid to go in. Too afraid of what I might find.

"My lord, answer me," I demanded, but there was no reply. "Grux! *Grivvux!* My Lord God, please say something, say anything!"

Only the mindless bluster of wind.

The door creaked as I opened it further and urged myself inside, but before I'd reached the bed, someone struck me from behind and the floor came swinging up to meet me, my head thudding painfully against the hardwood.

"I'm sorry, Sam," said his voice as he climbed over me, pinning me down. "This is the only way to save you!"

"What's happening?" I cried, flailing frantically until I managed to turn over. The eyes were all I could make out in the dark, so wide they seemed lidless. He began chanting in the ancient tongue, and the sacrificial blade winked in the moonlight as it rose over my chest. He drove it down, but I caught his wrist and held him off.

"We're out of time, Sam! This has to happen!"

"But I *served* you," I said, trying not to weep.

"Then *serve me*, Sam! This is for the greater good!"

The greater good ... I remembered the mandrake's sacrifice, how Grux couldn't just throw it in the fire. There were rules even he must obey. "You can't do this!" I screamed, feeling my heart pounding in my ears as the knife inched closer. "I don't agree to this! *Watchers!* I'm not a willing sacrifice!"

"Sam ..." he said, pressing down with all his strength, "*You're* not blameless." The knife jolted closer, its tip pressing into my shirt. "It's not your fault—it was never supposed to be you," he added, as if trying to comfort me before my murder. "There was no one else ... No one left."

Suddenly, I understood. I was only the Chosen One because I was the last. I wasn't *special*. Wasn't *holy*. Wasn't anything more than *here*.

I realized then that I hated him. I hated him for his power, and I hated him for his weakness. I hated him for what he gave and what he demanded. I should have known. Our own scripture tells us: *His right hand gives and his left hand takes, but his right hand also takes.*

With a sudden surge of determination, I pushed the knife from my chest and threw him off me. We struggled and writhed there on the floor, our bodies thumping against the hardwood.

"Sam!" he gasped. "*Please!* Think on what you do! Don't you want to save this world?"

He was stronger than I'd expected. I could barely hold him off.

The feathers …

Grux was stronger than me now, and he had the knife. He had everything he needed to save the world without me. Yet as we fought, he never swung or stabbed at me, but rather kept the blade tucked flat against his forearm, as if he was afraid of hurting me with it. I realized then that it was important to him that he kill me, but not hurt me.

That was his mistake.

I struck him as hard as I could across the cheek and then wrested the blade from his fumbling hand. Stunned, he reached after it wildly, cutting both hands before recoiling in fear. "Think of her!" he pleaded as I guided the blade over him. "You two were never meant to be forever, Sam! *This will be!*"

"I'm not doing this for her," I said through gritted teeth. "This is for me."

Grux gasped when the knife plunged through him. His lips trembled, searching for the words to undo this. "Oh, Sam," he said—not spitefully, but dripping with pity. "My poor lost child. There's no saving you now. There's no saving any of you ..."

Some last words.

It's been three weeks since I killed the one true god. Ellie's husband passed on the same day. I don't know if that's fate or coincidence, bad luck or nothing. Probably nothing, but then isn't everything?

We spoke once more in the days that followed. She's moving out of town, though she didn't say where she's going and I didn't ask. With the apocalypse on the horizon, I didn't think it mattered much.

"I hope you stay afloat," I told her.

She sniffled and cleared her throat. "I always do."

"No, I mean keep your raft handy."

She laughed and said goodbye.

I buried the Lord Most High in the backyard. He always liked to garden there. But now great thorny roses, bigger and brighter than any I've ever seen, have sprouted through the soft earth and spread through the yard. I don't know how they got there—if they were planted beforehand, or if they're the strange result of bird-magic leaving his body.

At first I ignored them, let them flourish like weeds before they finally tapped dry, their ruby petals wilting through the California drought. I had bigger concerns, after all. The crushing responsibility of the world's doom. The unknowable mystery that clung to my every thought: Did I betray God, or did God betray me?

It's not like I could pray about it.

I watched the world's end from my rooftop, the sun setting over an old world full of quiet joys, hidden griefs, petty and monstrous sins.

But the hour marked upon the cosmic calendar came and went unremarked. No rolling tide of judgment. No righteous annihilation. Maybe without God it couldn't happen. Or maybe the end is still coming and we just got the math wrong.

Maybe.

Maybe.

'Maybe' like the wet mortar around every brick of faith, waiting to harden into cold certainty. *It is not ours to know*, say the holy texts, *but to wait and see what God and fate have conspired.*

Wait and see, like a challenge.

Wait and see, like a threat.

I've started watering the roses at night, when it's cooler out. It's helped to break the habit of my evening prayers, the habit of kneeling and reaching out, only to receive the spiritual equivalent of a disconnect tone. And with Grux gone, a thought has been slowly boring into me:

There's no one to help us but us.

No sorrow or joy but us. No righteousness or sin but us.

The flowers have bounced back pretty quickly, their petals blood-bright, their leaves lush as Eden. My neighbor Penny loves them, and demanded to know my secret. I really didn't know what to tell her —I hadn't done anything special, hadn't applied arcane tricks or esoteric skills or a once in a generation green thumb.

"Care," I told her.

"That's usually what it comes down to," she said, and asked if I wouldn't mind helping her plant some in her own garden.

I've been going over every few days, first to plant the roses, then to help with other small tasks around the house. In turn, she's been showing me how to prune the flowers so they don't grow over each other, how to direct them so that they stay healthy and strong, how to water them at the right times to help with the drought.

"How's your father?" she asked the other day.

"Oh," I said awkwardly, "he actually passed a little while ago ..."

"I'm sorry to hear that, dear," she said. "He was a sweet man, I'm sure you miss him terribly. He's still with you though. I can feel him in you."

"Okay," I said, eager to drop it, hoping she was wrong, though a part of me hoped in spite of myself that she was right.

With her guidance, I've mulched and fertilized the soil around the rosebushes, even moved a few to keep them from crowding each other (or growing in the silhouette of a buried body). But the roses grow with a mind all their own, creeping with thorny vines across the yard to latch and climb the walls of the house. And each morning, their blushing, crimson faces turn not towards the rising sun but to my bedroom window, as if watching still for the coming of the lord.

See Hamilton Perez's story "Problems of the Flesh" online at Metaphorosis.
If you liked it, leave a comment. Authors love that!
Remember to subscribe to our e-mail updates so you'll know when new stories are posted.

About the story

I started this story around 2015 as a sort of final goodbye to the religious faith of my early adulthood. I thought it would be interesting if the Second Coming occurred, but rather than Christ returning in glory, he was weak or ill (though still supernatural). I didn't want to make the story about Christianity (or any particular religion), but rather about the challenges of faith, so I invented Grivvux, and Sam became a vehicle for me to explore what faith expects of us and what we expect of it.

A question for the author

Q: Are you an outline or discovery writer?

A: I've always been more of an outliner, but that's just another way to say that outlining is where I discover. Outlining lets me play with ideas freely, and it lets me jump around the story as things come to me.

That said, the actual writing/discover phase always changes the outline, so there's a lot of back and forth, which is probably why it takes me so long to finish anything. But it's the outlining that I enjoy most. That's where I get to play. The writing is where I work.

About the author

Hamilton Perez has been writing stories for as long as he can remember, and possibly even longer than that. His earliest known work is a fan-fiction crossover between *Star Wars, Terminator*, and *Jurassic Park*. It has yet to be picked up by a major studio, but Hamilton remains hopeful. When not writing, he can be found rolling 20-sided dice, playing irresponsibly with medieval weaponry, or chasing squirrels with the dog.

hamiltonperez.com, @TheWritingHam

A Xenothanatologist's Guidebook to Death Practices Among the Sapient Species of the Outer Perseus Arm of the Milky Way Galaxy

P.G. Streeter

Miri, I'm on my way.

My stomach has settled from that initial lurch of low-*g*. I've acclimated to my small cabin, and to the prospect of a long, lingering isolation.

It's quiet, and lonely, but I've nonetheless opted out of the long sleep of induced stasis. The cabin feels too much like a coffin as it is.

Here I am: alone, except for my precious few possessions, my thoughts—

—and *you*: the ghost I conjure from my deepest memories, a trick to keep myself sane.

Even though months will go by before this vessel approaches relativistic speeds, my sense of time's passage is already blurring. Suddenly, I find myself back in those fields, abandoned and overgrown, that stretched out between our childhood homes.

Do you remember them? It was in those tall, tangled grasses that we first met, first got into mischief.

Along the southern edge of that field, there was a river—mild in most seasons, but ferocious after the rainstorms that came in early spring. There, we'd swim.

I can hear your voice now, calling to me, beckoning me to join you where the current was strongest.

But I'm still afraid of those waters. I did not, *do not*, want to be swept away.

So, I refuse to follow the memory further. I grasp this hardbound book. I read.

Of the billions of star systems observed in the Milky Way's Outer Perseus Arm,

human starfarers have thus far discovered 83 that contain life-bearing planets or moons. On 27 of these worlds, we have found species whose intelligence rises to levels we can comfortably categorize as sapient.

This distinction is not always a straightforward one to make. Even when communication can be established, it is hard to gauge intelligence, *which frequently manifests in unexpected ways. Often, therefore, a vital factor in making such a determination has been the assessment made by the Terrestrial Guild of Xenothanatologists, whose members study alien species' attitudes toward death, and their treatment of the dead.*

After all, what could better inform us about species' humanity *than how they* conceptualize their mortality?

This guidebook will present a survey of xenothanatologists' initial findings in this region of the galaxy. These findings are not conclusive or all-encompassing, but the Company hopes they will give you, the budding xenothanatologist, a useful primer, here at the start of your promising career.

Do you insist on interrupting me, Miri?

Yes, I can hear your questions—or, rather, I feel them, like vibrations in the cabin's stale air. If I squint, I can almost see your lips parting as you speak, even if it's just a shimmer in my peripheral vision.

You wonder, of course, about the small marvel I'm clasping in my hands. *Hmm.* How can I explain the ways the world has changed since you've been gone?

When you left me, the world was on the cusp. I wonder if you anticipated the ways in which *Renew* would alter things—even as you refused its life-extending treatments.

Maybe you feared that the coming spike in population would outstrip the pace at which we built new habitats off-planet. Perhaps you worried about the *gap* —that rapidly widening gulf between those who had the means to receive the genetic therapy, and those who didn't.

I wish you had confided more in me, in the end—and I wish I could say I would've listened.

But I think some of the ways the world changed might genuinely have surprised you. For instance: technologies of convenience, such as those digital interfaces we'd gotten so accustomed to reading from, have fallen entirely out of fashion. I think this fact would have surprised me, too, if someone had told it to me during the first century or so of my life!

Now, items like physical, bound books, which take so much *time* to manufacture and get a hold of, are favored commodities. The reason for this is simple, really: now that our lives extend so many centuries, we have the luxury of 'taking it slow'. We *relish* those old technologies, precisely *because* they demand our time and patience. I think you would have liked that.

Of course, the Company would tell you that such things are 'wonderful reminders of our victory over death'. This, I suspect, you would have scoffed at.

This particular book—the guidebook I'm holding now—was one of the first readings assigned in my course of xenothanatological study. I've read it countless times, and, even though I've taken my studies far beyond its pages in the years since, it's still one of my favorites. It still reminds me of those first profound moments of inspiration it sparked in me—insights that I hope will lead me back to *you.*

If you read it with me, now, maybe you'll understand what it is I seek.

Countless cultural groups among the species we've observed follow death practices familiar to Earth-born humans. A plurality of xenocultures inter their dead, and nearly as many employ techniques akin to cremation.

On planets where fire is not a practical solution, we have observed the use of corrosives, voracious parasites, nanotechnology, and even mechanical grinding tools as methods for reducing a body to its component particles. Although some of the methodologies described above are somewhat disquieting to the human observer, their goals are clear, even relatable.

Yet some alien cultures we have encountered maintain thanatological practices that might shock, offend, or perplex those born of Earth. For instance, members of the Crustweaver religious sect on 16 Ellander b have an inviolable taboo against touching the deceased, directly or indirectly. Crustweavers use the dexterity of their long, spindly limbs to step over and around their dead, who are invariably left, unperturbed, in the exact spot where they expired.

The atmospheric conditions on 16 Ellander b, along with the physical makeup of the species' bodies, make for a slow decomposition process: it often takes the equivalent of 30-40 Earth years for a body to fully decompose. To compound the issue, this duration is roughly one-and-a-half times the length of the species' average lifespan. As a result, a Crustweaver who died at the moment of another Crustweaver's birth will likely not have fully decomposed by the time the latter deceases.

As can be imagined, the consequences of these practices are monumental. As Crustweaver communities continue to produce offspring faster than prior generations' bodies biodegrade, new generations find themselves among a landscape increasingly littered with their forebears' corpses.

The Crustweavers inhabit an isolated continent, as non-adherents to this sect's faith have long since learned to stay far away. In the Crustweavers' domain, the very shape of the world alters with each generation's passing. Yet, these pious beings manage to sidestep and squeeze past the dead that are scattered about their streets and homes.

They do so without trepidation or fear. In fact, they do not seem in the least perturbed by the slowly rotting remains of strangers and loved ones alike that pervade their world. They simply live their lives in a state of casual reverence to the fallen. Even as the world around them becomes crowded with cadavers, their taboo remains absolute.

In such cases, we are left to wonder how cultural exchange might even be possible between our people and theirs. However, the intrepid xenothanatologist finds a way.

Do you see the beads of sweat forming on my brow?

Yes, I realize it's quite cool in here. It's not heat, but a swell of dread that's causing me to perspire. The seed of a thought is sprouting in my mind. It's familiar, and unwelcome.

No, I don't wish to share it with you. Not now.

Besides, I can see it: the smirk on your face. Yes, Company texts such as this one love to make these sweeping statements. The intrepid xenothanatologist! I can see why you would find this amusing.

But don't give me that look! I understand that this is dripping with propaganda. I hope you don't assume I'm going into this endeavor with the naïve outlook of a younger man. After all, I'm decidedly *not* young. I haven't been for quite a long time.

Hmm. I'm scrambling to justify my actions, it seems. Is that why I've called upon your memory? Why I, the lifelong rationalist, have let myself get drawn into this game of make-believe?

So be it. I want to explain my choices, so explain them I *will.*

Why, after all, have I devoted myself to this Company's mission? Their job is to sell something, to spread *Renew* to other sapient species…at a cost. What does this act of commerce have to do with *me*?

It's simple: they *need* me—someone who can come to grips with these alien creatures' views on death. This is what

I've spent the last several years studying for, after all. And I've studied hard.

When I reach that understanding, my further job is to 'engender a dialogue' on the Company's behalf. I'm to build the cultural inroads needed to open up trade —and I'm sure I'll do so admirably.

None of this is the reason my confidence wavers. This isn't what's making me sweat.

What? Do you have to *needle* me like this? I'd almost forgotten how insistent you could be. But fine, *here*. I'll tell you what image has risen to my mind and made my heart start to beat so fast:

It's your hospice room—and you're no longer in it. They've just have wheeled you away. No—not *you*. The husk you left behind.

Do you see your belongings, scattered about the room? Piled clothes, half-unpacked bags, medical equipment that's still flashing as tubes and cords dangle about, untethered? This is the topography of the world you left behind.

The thought of such a world spurs my actions—but it also fills me with dread.

So, when I think about my mission— my *second* mission, the one I won't speak of out loud—I'm positively brimming with doubt. I'm afraid to talk about it even now —afraid even to whisper it to your ghost.

And although I'm still at the outset of my journey, visions of failure are already starting to cloud my thoughts. With each new world I visit, I'm afraid I'll only find one more empty promise. What if the answers I'm searching for never come?

For you, Miri, I'm still going to try. All I ask is that you bear with me.

Although the rationales behind some species' practices are opaque to our eyes, in many cases, attitudes surrounding death are easy to grasp. This is especially true when they are so clearly based on the biological necessities of the species' lives. Take, for instance, the Spin-Gliders of 44 Olivar c. Not unlike certain Earth sharks, these sky-dwelling creatures are obligate ram ventilators. That is, they must remain in constant motion for their respiratory systems to function.

The flyers spend their waking lives swooping and diving along the gas giant's hydrogen currents, and the species has even mastered a technique by which they can sleep for short stints while caught in a spiraling gust of hot air. It is astonishing that such beings have developed rich culture and technology while living a life constrained by the need for constant motion; yet, they have done so.

Of course, the only way to come to anything like a complete rest on a planet with no solid surface is to descend to the stratum of liquid hydrogen closer to the planet's core.

The majority of the planet's cultural groups therefore honor their dead in this fashion: they carry them to this liquid surface. Rather than simply allowing them to drop, they take great care to lay their dead upon buoyant, gyroscopically stabilized platforms. Here, no winds carry them, no waves buffet them about. So it is that a Spin-Glider comes to a state of rest only upon death.

If life is motion, then how better to acknowledge—and ultimately accept—its absence, than to create a condition of perfect stillness?

Is that what death is for you, Miri? Stillness?

I can close my eyes, clutch this book to my chest, concentrate on breathing, and know that this brief *pause* doesn't mean the *end*.

But what's your perspective on the matter? No flights of fancy, no phantoms created by my imagination, will ever give me access to *that* knowledge.

If only you could tell me! After all, you've read much of the same old literature that I have. How many times has that phrase appeared—reference to the 'stillness of the grave'? We grew up in a world where that outcome was an inevitability. And, yet, in your final years, even you knew that it didn't have to be. Not anymore.

For a long time, humanity either accepted the idea that one day all we'd come to rest—or hoped against hope that, in some invisible way, life kept going. Those seemed to be the only options.

But when *Renew* became a reality, things changed: we didn't have to resign ourselves to nothingness or place our hopes in some unknown 'hereafter'. We could continue to live, in the here and now! I saw this, saw the gift it offered us. So why couldn't I persuade *you* to embrace that change as well?

It's ironic, I suppose, that this act of persuasion—the *sales pitch*—is my job now. I study how people on faraway worlds conceptualize death, all so that the Company can sell them *life*.

You'd laugh, I think, to hear about the team I'm a part of. I swear, they stick the prefix *xeno* on any and every old job title, any time alien cultures are involved. There are *xenoeconomists* to negotiate the terms of the trade, and *xenobiologists*, who figure out how to adapt *Renew*'s life-extending biotech to other species' physiology.

And then, there's me: the one who is trusted, above all others, to discover the terms under which our product will be most desirable to our strange new friends.

Me, the person who failed so utterly to convince you that a long life was worth living.

Of course, it is not only the handling and disposal of physical corpses with which the xenothanatologist is concerned. She must ask, how do different xenocultures talk about their dead? How do they memorialize them?

Eulogies and obituaries are prevalent among virtually all literate species in this region of the galaxy. Many deliver short orations or produce written tributes after a loved one's passing, much as Earth humans have historically done. However, many have practices that go much further.

Consider the denizens of 6 Aleska e. You have likely read about this species, for their body plan is famously far closer to Earth humans' than any other extraterrestrial life yet discovered. That is, they have an ovoid head, a neck, torso, and limbs both fore and hind. Further, they walk on these hind legs and reserve the fore for tool use.

While these likenesses are truly extraordinary, it is here that their similarities to our kind end. They have no mouths, no visible organs of hearing or olfaction; their eyes, while prominent, do not resemble our own, but instead consist of a complex beehive of chromelike surfaces that stretch around their heads' circumference.

They go about naked, their pale skin exposed at all times, and it is on this blank canvas that their method of communication emerges. Through a shifting set of luminescent cells just under their outer dermis, these Skinwriters communicate. Intricate images in vibrant colors shift across their bodies, allowing for a complex visual language.

When a Skinwriter dies, its flesh returns to neutral pale tones. It is then that the Artists of the Dead set to work: first, preserving the deceased's body, then inscribing a series of fine tattoos over the entirety of their skin's canvas.

Here is the Skinwriter's epitaph: a pictogrammatic account of the deceased's life, told from birth to death. The craftsmanship of this body art, along with the level of detail recollected in its lines and colors, becomes a permanent tribute to the deceased, displayed forever in a glass mausoleum. A hastily tattooed corpse, or one whose pictograms tell a vague or incomplete story, reveals a life unsatisfactorily lived. Yet, if one's preserved corpse becomes a true work of art, such is the ultimate testament to that person's life.

I was asked, of course, to speak at your funeral. I wrote your obituary—*that* was easy enough. There's a formula there, one

I didn't need to stray from. Your life, your education, your accomplishments—all of it lined up into easy paragraphs! I let these simple, reductive facts flow onto the page, all the way to the last sentence, the one that lists the people you've left behind.

Of course, with no children, with your parents and brothers already gone, this left only *me.*

So, yes, I composed the necessary words—and several old friends even reached out to tell me how touching my tribute was.

But when they asked me to *speak*, there was only emptiness inside me, in those deep places where I'd expected to find inspiration.

Were you there, Miri? A true ghost, listening intently for the words I would utter in your honor? Were you ashamed, then, when all I could do was stand there and openly weep?

Do I see you turning your eyes away from me, even now?

Stay with me for a while, I'm begging you. We're getting closer and closer to the questions that have led me to this ship— that have led me across the stars in search of you.

Two species should be further noted for the unique roles language takes in referring to the dead. The first, the insectiform Fim of 19 Magna k have a rich spoken language, a series of chirps and clicks that has led to a wealth of literary art. Yet, the language has a surprising gap: there are no names for the living, no way to refer to other Fim at all.

Their language allows for discussion of the self—of their natural world and their interactions with it, of their desires, and of their own past actions. It likewise has a version of the word you *—a way to indicate the speaker's direct audience. But, whether because of an evolutionary quirk of neurology or through a deeply ingrained social practice, a Fim cannot, when talking to a compatriot, refer to a third person and her actions.*

That is, they cannot do so until a fellow Fim dies. At this point, her deeds are proclaimed loudly and often. The dead Fim is named immediately—and without deliberation—and that name is, by means of some mechanism we do not yet understand, immediately known to all.

In death, a Fim's story, impossible to discuss during her life, becomes a legend widely told.

As improbable as it seems, 23 Argen c contains a population of beings, the aquatic Kell, whose sociolinguistic response to death is precisely the opposite of the Fims': when a Kell dies, it is, to the remainder of this species, as if he never existed at all.

Upon death, the body begins to sink to the bottom of the planet's highly acidic oceans. Though a living Kell's body produces enzymes which protect him from the corrosive waters, this production stops at death. So, as the dead Kell's body sinks, it quickly begins to disintegrate.

Simultaneously, all other Kell begin to act as if their friend or family member never existed. The requisite vocabulary is no longer available.

In the Company's attempts to communicate about this phenomenon, references to the dead Kell by human translators led to consistently perplexed responses.

Do the Kell immediately forget their dead, or do they act out of strict custom? If the latter, what value system led to such a practice? If the former, then what are the implications for the Kell worldview?

Though results are preliminary, our initial outreach group has hypothesized that the Kell are not aware of death's existence at all. Those who live, live. That is all they know.

How can I make you understand how it was for me, Miri? Once you were gone, it was like the truth of your life had become utterly inarticulable.

How could I bring your name from my lips into the world, when the empty space you left was so vast? Any feeble vibrations I attempted to speak into that void would be meaningless, incomplete. They would not be *you*, which means they would be an insult to your memory.

It all sounds extreme, doesn't it? But losing you *was* such an extreme thing to experience. You were there, a part of my life—and then you weren't.

And it only got worse. I kept telling people that I wanted to 'honor your memory', but I soon found myself asking what *memory* was even worth. Every day that passed without you in it, I dissociated even further, to the point where I soon found myself disbelieving my own recollections.

In the wake of your loss, I was unmoored from reality. What was real, I wondered, and what was the fiction I'd created to soothe myself, to make the grief easier to bear? This is the spiral I was caught up in, the state of total panic that consumed me: one where memory was a lie, and every word I uttered was a failed attempt to bring you back.

I felt despair, but I never questioned my choice to embrace extended life. I couldn't allow myself to be erased from the world the same way you had been.

Yet, where could I go from there?

The answer, as I'm sure you've guessed, began to take shape when I first read this book.

Do I sound obsessive? I suppose I must. I became fixated on the idea of finding some alien culture whose views on death might offer me reassurance. When presented, for instance, with the discovery of a species who forget their dead entirely, I found myself wondering if *this* was the solution. Could I abandon your memory, washing you clean from my thoughts so that I wouldn't have to keep shouldering the burden of your loss?

Ultimately, I rejected this notion. It was unseemly, perverse even.

I also quickly discarded any answers rooted in superstition—all those traditions proclaiming a spiritual afterlife. These were untestable, un*knowable*. They were a sign of epistemic defeat, acts of faith I could never commit to.

Still, now that I had started along this path, I was determined to discover *something* out there: some creature in the far-flung cosmos who could offer me solace.

So, my choice was made: I would become a xenothanatologist. I would even sell myself to this Company if that's what it took. I would become the human ambassador to the dead of other worlds.

And, perhaps, I started to realize, to worlds like *ours*: ones that had left death *behind*.

A society's practices surrounding death will necessarily change when that society makes the concept of 'natural death' obsolete. Earth humans, of course, encountered this reality upon the invention of Renew. *Unsurprisingly, other species in*

the cosmos have also discovered a measure of immortality, whether through natural or technological means.

Still, it's rare to find a species that truly fits the description of biological immortality. On Earth, non-sapient species such as lobsters, whose production of the enzyme telomerase allows for unending cell regeneration, are close to achieving such a descriptor. In fact, Renew is itself partly inspired by such beings: one important component of the treatment is the prevention of telomere shortening as cells regenerate. However, it is worth noting that while such species do not die by aging, their lives, just as ours, might easily be cut short due to violent means.

On 8 Alma n, a sapient species appears to have achieved such biologically immortal status. The species—whom we call Stonediggers—have nigh-impenetrable rocklike exteriors. They do not require air to breathe, nor any form of sustenance other than exposure to sunlight. Further, they can store an excess of solar energy that lasts for weeks on end, so death due to solar deprivation is an unlikely outcome. In short, they are virtually unkillable. Like lobsters or Renew-enhanced humans, they do not age in any recognizable sense; the *oldest among them, by Company reckoning, has been alive for nearly twelve million Earth years.*

Elsewhere, technological means have extended other species' lifespan greatly. One such example hails from 1 Hemnes d. There, the Bright Ones claim to have developed the means by which to preserve a dying person's conscious mind and transfer it to a new, synthetic host body. The process, they claimed, might be repeated indefinitely, with perfect fidelity—nothing lost in the transfer.

While similar techniques had been attempted on Earth before Renew was perfected, humankind had concluded that the consciousness could not survive the transfer process.

Here, though, we found a fully functioning society of techno-organic beings. Upon first contact, Company representatives determined they would need to investigate further: could this technique supplement our existing life-extending biotechnology?

Can you see them, Miri—the thoughts that have begun to take shape in my mind? I picture you leaning in, listening more attentively than before.

These are the stories, you see, that tantalize me above all others, even if all they provide me with are false glimpses of hope. I really am enthusiastic—practically *evangelical*—about *Renew* and the extended life it offers, but the simple fact is that no matter how far we reach across the cosmos, there is one place we will never be able to spread this technology.

We can't bring it to the *past*. We can't offer it to those whose lives ended before it arrived, nor to those who stubbornly refused its miracle.

Again, you smirk. You're shaking your head—yes, I can see it, no matter how subtle you think you are.

But hear me out, please. Ask, as I did, whether there is a solution here. Can the promise of recovering and transferring a conscious mind offer the missing piece? Not for those of us who already have *Renew* coursing through our veins, but for those who are already gone?

What would it take to retrieve a mind that was lost *long ago*? Could such a person's consciousness be pulled from the ether, brought back into existence?

I imagine your eyes getting wide at this —but don't get your hopes up just yet.

With such questions in mind, Company representatives sought to learn how the Bright Ones' transfer process worked. For how long, post-expiry, might a consciousness be retrieved from the deceased's brain? Does the process involve the transfer of brain tissue itself into the new host body, or are memories and perspectives translated to a new medium?

As it turns out, this purported transfer of consciousness was not what the Bright Ones initially advertised.

A look into the species' past reveals the full story. The Bright Ones long ago developed infinitesimally small surveillance devices—quantum drones— that, produced on a massive scale, began to observe all life across their planet, at all times. All was known; no knowledge was kept secret.

Using the vast data gathered, the engineers of 1 Hemnes d were able to create intricately complex models of a deceased Bright One's mind, informed by the full set of objective experiences encountered over a lifetime. The internal perspective was not retained—only inferred—but these inferences were made with a nuanced understanding of Bright One psychology, and were therefore arguably quite accurate.

Yet, it cannot be denied that the deceased person's consciousness was not, in fact, preserved. When one of these biological persons died, their mind was merely recreated. No matter how accurate, it was but a replica. As such, the original beings that once inhabited this land slowly died off, only to be replaced by new, synthetic beings. At some point in the distant past, the last biological Bright One expired. All that remains are their algorithmic replacements, the computer-modeled copies of the deceased.

How could a species have allowed this to occur? Was it merely that, in their inability to cope with the absence of departed loved ones, the Bright Ones decided their simulated presence would suffice? Perhaps only a select few knew the process to be fraudulent, and the masses were merely fooled. We do not yet know the answer.

Although the Company has come to recognize artificial intelligence as true life, *the fact remains, nonetheless, that these creatures are not genuine* continuations *of the lives that had come before.*

In the meantime, subsequent visits to 8 Alma n revealed that their story, as well, is more complicated than initially perceived. For one, the appellation given— Stonediggers—in truth applies only to one faction of the species. It remains in use by Earth humans due to its widespread early adoption; however, the differences between the two main factions are worth exploring.

For example, when members of that first faction—the true *Stonediggers—come of age, they are known to retreat to isolated places, where they build massive stone shelters and spend their endless lives making little contact with others. On rare occasions, Stonediggers seek partners for mating, but any pairings formed for this purpose last only until their offspring reach maturity.*

Only when we met the second faction, called Sun-Sailors, did we learn an astonishing truth: the species, no matter the faction, are not *solitary by disposition. In fact, many Stonediggers find the condition of isolation to be torturous. What circumstances, then, might have led these virtually invincible giants to take such extreme precautions against harm?*

The Sun-Sailors offered us an explanation for their cousins' behavior: since death is so rare, it is vastly more traumatic than it would be in a world where it is commonplace. Therefore, a segment of the species' population began to take hyperbolic measures to prevent death's occurrence.

Sun-Sailors eschew this philosophy. They live their lives freely, knowing that they will likely persist for millennia—or more—but that, against the backdrop of infinity, the mathematical odds of a tragic demise creep ever closer to 1.

The wisest of the Sun-Sailors insist that even those who persist for billions of years will do so only to one day meet their end as the universe collapses into itself.

Asked about their appellation, the Sun-Sailors revealed something even more astonishing: namely, that it is not uncommon, after several hundred millennia of life, for a Sun-Sailor to quietly walk away from their community and seek out the planet's only functional spaceport. The small craft launched from this port are calibrated for a single destination: their system's fiery yellow star.

For such a one, no funeral services are held, no songs sung. But those who perform this act are nonetheless spoken of with quiet respect: they have confronted the one thing in so long a life that remains unknown, that remains unknowable.

Miri, even though my body feels young—and I suppose it *looks* that way to you, too—I've never felt more aware of how *old* I truly am. In fact, I'm the oldest by far aboard this Company ship.

I'm the only one here who remembers a time when human death was something certain, a mundane occurrence.

To the others, it's some improbable, tragic 'maybe' that can be escaped for centuries on end. They're like the Sun-Sailors: death doesn't weigh heavily on their hearts and minds. They don't seek it out—but it also doesn't dwell with them constantly, as it does with me.

They don't whisper in the dark to someone lost to them long ago; they don't play host to ghosts.

They don't have *you.*

So, while they simply try to sell a product, I look into the cracks and crevices of every new society we find. I study their rituals, their stories, their technology, looking for the one thing we haven't been able to create:

The way to bring someone back.

That's why, until we make planetfall, I'm determined to pore over this book's pages, again and again. I'm desperate to uncover something new.

What is it? Is that your hand I feel, resting on mine? It's still a struggle to see you, to perceive your touch. But it feels like you're guiding my hands, compelling me to riffle backward through these pages. Miri, what I have missed?

Here. Two pages stuck together. What will we find hidden between them?

Maybe we can discover it together.

A small number of social groups among the Spin-Gliders of 44 Olivar c *take a different tack entirely.*

Rather than allowing their dead a final stasis upon the hydrogen seas below, the citizens of these communities carry their lost loved ones to the globe-spanning windstreams found in the upper atmosphere. Released here, the body of a dead Spin-Glider will be pulled into motion perpetually.

Where there is motion, they argue, there is life.

Living Spin-Gliders cannot join their fallen among these winds: the gusts are violent and strong, and they would whip a living soul away from the world he knew in no time at all.

The second life they release their loved ones to is therefore necessarily a mystery to them; they cannot join until their own time comes. But they believe, with every ounce of their being, that it is real—that they have conquered death.

Is this what you would show me, Miri? A 'second life'—a spiritual mystery?

You know me well enough to realize how hard a pill that is for me to swallow. I don't *do* spirituality; I can't wrap my mind around faith.

Please—don't mock me. Yes, I know. Even now, I'm talking to your ghost. But I'm no fool: I know what you are. You're a child's fantasy, conjured from my memories, the product of my brokenness.

Even as I acknowledge this, you fade from me. Don't go!

Stay with me, and remember, Miri. Remember our field, our river—how only you were strong enough to brave those currents.

I can picture it now: the day when, despite my cries and protests, you let it sweep you away, hollering gleefully as it carried you downstream. We both knew what awaited: a steep ledge overlooking a reservoir. You'd argued again and again that the waters were deep, that the waterfall would carry us safely over. The ten-foot freefall would be a momentary thrill, followed by a refreshing *splash.*

You were fully prepared to take that leap.

But you heard my shouts of protest—or perhaps caught a glimpse of my panicked face as I ran alongside the river after you —and you grabbed a tree root that jutted from the bank. You held on.

When I pulled you out, you said, between shivers, that you wouldn't do it again—not if I wouldn't go with you.

Decades later, though, you let time's river pull you away, even though I refused to follow.

What's worse, Miri, is that you didn't *need* to. Yes, I know: *Renew* was still so new when you got sick—but I'd saved enough money for us *both* to begin the treatment. It was *not* too late.

Yet you just smiled and shook your head, refusing without spoken justification, even knowing that I'd already begun to let it rewrite my own genetics.

And then, you were gone.

Now, I swear I will find you again.

Rivers, skies, worlds of rock and sun and blustering gusts of hydrogen. I look for you in these places.

Deep down, I know my motivations are selfish. You've gone somewhere I don't dare follow, and so, a coward to the end, I look for a way to bring *you* back to *me*.

Knowing all of this, I look out my vessel's starboard window, awaiting the light of alien suns...

I'll sail on past them. I'll traverse this void as far as I must go—carried through the infinite cosmos as if caught in a river's current.

See P.G. Streeter's story "A Xenothanatologist's Guidebook to Death Practices Among the Sapient Species of the Outer Perseus Arm of the Milky Way Galaxy" online at Metaphorosis.
If you liked it, leave a comment. Authors love that!
Remember to subscribe to our e-mail updates so you'll know when new stories are posted.

About the story

A friend of mine recently earned a degree in the field of thanatology—the study of death. I was fascinated to learn about this discipline, and I even imagined that if I were to go back in time to repeat my own years in academia, I might choose to study this subject myself. But, as it is, I've made a career of teaching literature and a hobby of dabbling in some writing of my own. So, I asked: how could I take this idea and apply it to a bit of speculative fiction?

Of course I immediately began imagining alien creatures, and how their own views on death might be shaped by the unique circumstances of their physiology and planetary ecology. The textbook sections of this story started coming to me, and I furiously started to put them to paper.

Attempting to make the personal narrative underpinning all of this work just as well was much more difficult. I knew I needed this part to be more emotional, whereas the textbook portions were intellectual. The narrator needed to be grappling with death on a personal level, and that story needed to resonate with those informational passages in a coherent way. Honestly, though, this was really hard! I'm infinitely grateful to B. Morris Allen, whose guidance during the revision process really helped me make that story come to life so much more strongly than it did in earlier drafts.

The universe is big, and I have no doubt that there's other intelligent life out there. I don't know how those beings conceptualize mortality—but I do know that confronting the reality of death can be a harrowing personal journey. The more I look beyond the initial perspectives I learned by rote as a child—the more I turn to the wisdom of people across different disciplines and from different cultures—the more comfortable I get with the ultimate mystery of it all. Years ago, trying to tell this story would have put me into a state of perpetual heebie-jeebies. Somehow, though, I've gotten to a place where this story was exceedingly fun to write. It's the fun that comes from being curious about ideas, from allowing yourself to luxuriate in questions of what if. Art, and especially fiction, have helped me get there. I hope that, among whatever else it made you think and feel, this story invoked a bit of that curiosity in you, too--and that you had a bit of fun staring into the abyss with me.

A question for the author

Q: How often do you think about writing during a day?

A: Some part of my scattered, overactive mind is probably always thinking about writing, but I've worked really hard to reign that in, and to put those thoughts on hold until an appropriate time arises. Because of this, my phone is full of notes with little snippets of ideas—new premises, story titles, character names, and bits of dialogue that I plan to come back to later. The surfaces of my house are littered with sticky notes and scraps of paper that serve the same purpose. Much of it doesn't end up getting used, but most of the stories I've gotten published these last few years owe themselves in part to those notes. The notes are important for another reason: if I simply dropped everything to write whenever the fancy struck me, I'd probably get fired from my dayjob—and my wife and kids would be pretty grumpy, too.

About the author

P.G Streeter lives with his wife and two sons in Maryland, where he teaches high school English and philosophy. He writes speculative fiction because he can't figure out any other way to get all the strange and disturbing dreams out of his head.

pgstreeter.wordpress.com/publications, @p_g_sWrites

Holding On

Justen Russell

I was eight years old when Yuri Zhilin floated away.

Yuri, the first man to orbit Io; the first human to walk on Ganymede. Replacing the lens of the JUVENTAS orbital telescope was supposed to be a routine procedure. Something done a half-dozen times with a half-dozen other telescopes around the closer planets and their moons. It wasn't even the first untethered spacewalk over Jupiter; Mimi Lin had beaten him to that almost a year earlier.

Still, I *had* to watch. It was Yuri.

I'd sucked up to José all week so we could watch the broadcast together on his father's new omniscreen. At that resolution we could count the stitches under Yuri's ROSCOSMOS badge—four: one for each planet he had orbited. Of course, I was more interested in his hair. Six long, straw-blond strands had escaped the bun on the back of Yuri's head and, without gravity to restrain them, they danced. Hairs just like mine.

Before his spacewalk, Yuri gave a tour of the capsule where he and Mimi had spent the past seven years. He showed the workstations filled with experiments, the sleeping harnesses, and what counted as a toilet in zero g. "Study hard, earthlings," he said in his thick Russian accent, "and you can be like us." José and I, we believed him too.

At the cockpit, Mimi Lin waved for the camera and, for perhaps the first time in my life, I understood what it meant to be jealous. I would have given anything to be her then, to have floated next to Yuri just once.

While he suited up, Yuri explained in Russian the purpose of everything he would wear. Gloves, belt, boots, I caught the main words—just not the small ones in between. José and I would use those same words when we played to make it more authentic. Like it was possible for us to work for ROSCOSMOS too.

Yuri's helmet had its own internal camera and when he put it on, his face appeared as a small inset in the bottom right-hand corner of our screen—smiling as always. He blew a kiss to the Earth, then pushed himself towards the airlock.

Ten meters of open space separated their capsule from the orbital telescope. Any closer and the protective magnetic field of their spacecraft would have damaged the satellite's delicate sensors. Ten meters exactly—no give or take. Mimi Lin held them in perfect alignment.

Yuri had one hundred and eighty-nine successful spacewalks on his record. I knew that number by heart. It was twenty-six more than Mimi Lin. It was nearly double the third place. One hundred eighty-nine times, Yuri Zhilin had stepped out into the void, then on the one hundred and ninetieth his mind shut down.

I could tell something was wrong the moment he pushed off, even before his arms started to flail, even before his legs started to kick. His eyes, so clear in that ultra-high definition inset in the bottom right corner of our screen, went blank. Yuri was no longer there.

With a forty-three-minute speed-of-light delay, there was nothing anyone on earth could do except watch. Whatever would happen already had. Mimi Lin had left the cockpit and hesitated at the airlock; she had suited up, calculated trajectories, and then suited back down. Twenty minutes before we watched Yuri kick off, she had concluded what we were about to: Yuri Zhilin was already gone.

'Space Sickness', the TV commentator explained after the 'live' broadcast cut out. It would become the new word of the summer. 'A rare catatonic response to stimulatory overload in high stress situations.' It was nearly unheard of among professional astronauts, but everyone knew they were the minority in space. Among the asteroid miners and orbital laborers—well—no one kept statistics on them, but 'Space Sickness', we would learn, probably claimed more than half. Outer space was littered with the bodies of those who couldn't quite hold on; usually, they were not broadcast for the whole world to see.

My mother named me Laika after the Russian dog that went to space. I think she meant it to be aspirational. *A stray who made it to the stars.* No one ever told her that the dog died on the way up. No one tells a woman like my mother things that might ruin her smile.

She left Quito for Manta when they started building the elevator. It was a good time to be a woman with a smile like hers. The streets there were full of contractors, astrophysicists, and astronauts, all with good jobs and full pockets. Back before the gated communities went up, and Manta became another Quito on the sea. Even Yuri passed through on his way up.

She said my father was an astronaut named Mudak. She used to tell me he was where I got my blonde hair. There is no way she could have known for sure—there were a lot of blond foreigners in Manta—but if I was going to have a fake father, he might as well have been an astronaut.

I always knew there was a real Mudak —whether he was my father or not. My mother could not have made up a name like that. See, people did not tell my mother things, but they told me. Things like 'Laika died on the way up' and 'a mutt's name suits a *mulatta* like you'.

Things like 'you know *mudak* means testicle in Russian, right?'.

Mudak is like calling someone an asshole. *Mudak* is calling someone a jerk. Usually, *mudak* is what you call a person you don't like, but sometimes Mudak is how another *mudak* introduces his friend when they are trying to be funny and don't want to give a real name to the smiling girl.

I don't know if Mudak really was an astronaut, or if he just wanted to see more than a smile. I don't know if he really was my father, or just the best *mudak* around the right time. All the men my mother smiled at were *mudaks*, but if she had any regrets, she never told me. The *mudaks* kept us fed. At least, they used to.

I never had a smile like my mothers, even before I lost three teeth fighting over something silly like my father and his name, but that did not matter, because I was going to space. Sometimes after I fought, I would tell my mother I had tripped; that I wasn't meant for gravity. She liked that too. "Just like your father," she would say, and I think she meant it—not like the other mothers. The ones who say, "Yes darling, someday you will have a mansion on the hill," because they know that the day their child finally understands, she will have grown up and no longer needs her mother.

For my mom, there was always something romantic about the elevator. It was never just another feature along the horizon. The wind turbines, the luxury cruise liners, the mansions on the hill—those were meant for *mudaks* and not for us. The mutt never gets invited inside, but there is room for her on a rocket, if she isn't concerned about coming back.

In the morning, when the sun shone from the east and the sky was clear, you could see the elevator—a thin, silver thread reflecting the light, stretched taut from heaven to horizon. At night, some trait of the filament in the upper atmosphere caused it to glow—the *equatorial aurora*—and a dancing line of green and purple floated in front of the stars. Most of the time, however, the cable itself was too far away and too thin to see.

Only the crawlers were visible when, for José's tenth birthday, his father drove us to San Mateo, where the cliffs overlooked the ocean. Before the elevator, he'd read, astronauts used to train on special parabolic flights. Ones that fly high in the sky then nose-dive straight down so the passengers inside can feel what it is like to be without gravity. They still did, I told him, just as children, not astronauts-to-be. The first time Yuri floated was at a birthday party where the parents had rented a parabolic plane; but our cliffs would be just as good.

"We will float for two whole seconds," José said. He had done the math and knew that part for sure. "Just like Yuri," he added for me.

We raced up the cliffs, each of us eager to be the first to jump, but in the end, it was José's birthday and I let him win. Only, after he leapt, I didn't; I couldn't.

I remember wanting to. I had been excited, even as José's scream echoed off the water below. But then I walked to the edge to make sure the landing was clear. I don't remember if it was. I just remember how much taller that cliff looked from the top, and how very, very far away the ocean seemed.

José hollered for me to jump. Then, he climbed back up and tried to convince me that it would be okay. It wasn't me that needed convincing, it was my legs; they wouldn't co-operate. They wouldn't step. I wanted to jump. At least, I wanted to *have* jumped, but I couldn't make myself approach that void.

When he could wait no longer, José left me there. He jumped again, and again, and again—and I didn't.

Each time, José was fine. It was me, still at the top, who was broken. I had to climb back down the way I had come up.

José didn't yell at me for ruining his birthday. He pretended we had both had fun, but I cried that night because I knew I would never be a Yuri, or a Mimi—or even brave like my mother when she left everything she had known for a new city. I would never be able to jump.

The next morning my mother wiped away my tears and marched me all the way back to the cliffs. It took hours to get there on foot, but she said, "Trust me." And I did.

We climbed the rocks together—slowly this time—and she stood with me at the top, all the way back from the edge. She said, "Sometimes, when you know what you have to do, it is better not to look." Then she grabbed my hand and said, "Close your eyes," and we ran. We didn't look and we didn't stop, we just fell off the edge of the world, and for two full seconds we were weightless in the air.

I jumped off the cliff a second time, and third, and a fourth—until my mother said we had to go back because the sun would soon disappear. It was easier every time. By the end of the day, it no longer mattered if I ran or if I looked. My legs kept working.

My mother laughed the whole way home—about the way I had screamed in the air, about the way my arms and legs had flailed when I fell. It didn't matter; I had jumped. I laughed about my flailing arms too.

Her smile always made everything okay. I wish I could have learned to smile like my mother, to have given that back to her just once before I left.

'Study hard, earthlings,' Yuri had said, 'and you can be like me.' José, maybe; he had it all planned out, every step required for a documented position at the top. Scholarship to a secondary school on the hill, two years of college outside Manta, engineering degree from the University in another three. He would never be an astronaut—ROSCOSMOS didn't scout for people like us—but he could get up the elevator, so long as his father sold their house to afford tuition. It wouldn't be grades that held him back.

My mother didn't have a house to sell. She had a smile, and every year, it seemed, fewer and fewer men smiled back. Maybe it was the whisper of wrinkles around her eyes, or maybe just the way a city changes, but my mother had started smiling at men she would have never smiled at before. Men who were not good to be around when the smiling stopped.

I used to dream that someday she would only need to smile at me. I would come back and look after her the way she had looked after me; we would hold on together. I knew it would never happen. The best I could dream was that she would no longer need to look after me—a girl who would never smile like my mother could.

I started standing at the docks near the unemployed women and men, waiting for my way out. While José was studying, and the children on the hill played, I pretended I was watching the elevator; but I liked to go best when the weather was bad, when even the crawlers were hard to see.

The docks were less crowded when it rained, and I would think, *Maybe if there is no one else, someone will choose me.* If a boat came by looking for workers, I would puff out my chest and stand on my toes to look strong and tall. Then, I would keep staring where the crawlers should be, even as the boat left.

That is why Belen chose me. She was looking at the elevator too.

"We'll get close enough to touch it," she told me. "If that's what you want." She was tall, and far too thin, with dark curly hair and a frown that said she understood.

She told her captain she'd chosen me instead of a big man with arms the size of tree trunks because, "She'll eat less." He shrugged and wiped the rain from his bald head, then told us both to help him unload.

I'd gotten lucky. You have to get lucky to make it to space. Even Yuri was a backup on his first mission, until the main pilot caught the flu. Before that he was just a *mudak* looking up.

From the shore, the wind turbines had always seemed small. Like the yachts and mansions that also decorated the horizon, they were just toys. Simulacra that filled the ocean between the mainland and the Galapagos, sprouting from the water like reeds in a pond. I used to think, *How can those hoist ten-tonne rockets into space?*

On the rusted *Buena Mañana*, as we floated directly beneath one, the sun flickered in the shadows of its whirring blades, each two hundred meters across. I was almost afraid to see the elevator the same way; afraid and excited. It would be real then. Would I still be willing to leap?

"Mussels will grow anywhere," Belen told me, as she zipped the wetsuit up to my neck. "Hanging out here, where there are no starfish or crabs, they get big."

The elevator had dispensed with the need for rocket fuel—at least at launch— but the crawlers that climbed along it needed energy to reach space. Energy supplied by the wind through those turbines and the massive electric cables that stretched out between them under the sea. As Belen explained, there were mussels growing in long, cylindrical nets called *socks* that dangled all along each cable's length.

"Haru buys them as *seed*," she said. That's what you call juvenile mussels, when they are just large enough to start clumping together—about half the length of a fingernail—mussel seed. Any smaller and they would slip right through the mesh of the *socks*.

"Nine months after we hang them, they are big enough to harvest," Belen said. "That's where we come in. Someone needs to dive down and hook the *socks*, so the crane can haul them up. Don't worry; you'll love it. The open ocean is just like outer space."

She had helmets to make me believe her. Tucked in a locker along the side of the fishing trawler were eight flawless, glassy orbs. Space helmets, exactly as I had seen them in countless magazines and low res-feed. Helmets just like Yuri's, save, of course, the ROSCOSMOS lettering.

"They used to make them in Manta," Belen said, "so, we find plenty floating out here. They work the same in zero bar or ten, so might as well use them diving."

"They float?"

"Would you believe that some people try to ride up outside the elevator with just a helmet and an air tank?" Belen said. "I don't know what they think they'll do after they make it to the top." She chose a small helmet for me to try on. "When they are sitting up there in outer space in a t-shirt and shorts, but they never make it that far anyway. Not with a diving regulator connecting the helmet to the tank."

The helmet felt tight around the neck, but Belen seemed happy with that. "A good seal," she said, "will keep the water out. But a diving regulator," she clipped the helmet in place, "that's what puts air there in the first place. It *regulates* how fast air comes out of the tank. It's designed to match the pressure around it. That way you can breathe when the weight of the entire ocean is trying to squeeze you. In higher pressure water, it delivers higher pressure air. Thing is, at least for the people trying to ride on top of a climber, when there is no pressure around it, a diving regulator won't deliver any air at all ... or maybe the valves freeze?" She hesitated, trying to figure out exactly how someone would die in her hypothetical. "Either way, no air. They pass out halfway up and fall. The water around us is littered with their bodies, and their helmets."

"How *do* you make it up then?" I asked.

"That's the silly part," Belen said. "They want us up there—the companies at least. Nothing is locked. If you pick the right crawler, you can seal yourself inside and ride all the way to space. Most of the floaters out here never had a plan, and never had a chance. But us—it'll be different for us."

I didn't miss her choice of words: *us*.

"From up close, we'll be able to read the logos," Belen said, choosing a helmet for herself. "The mining crawlers are the good ones. Anglo American, Ferrobras New Horizon, Objectif Outre-Terre. The last few times it's been NASA and CNSA. Can't stow away with astronauts."

It hadn't occurred to me to be picky about what spaceship I ended up on. "Why not?" I asked.

"Pick the wrong crawler and it's out the airlock," Belen snapped her fingers, "like that!" Then she laughed. I couldn't tell if she was serious or not.

If anything, the ocean was the opposite of space. At least, the opposite of what I expected space would be. Space was open.

Space was empty. Whenever Yuri left his capsule, every star had been visible from light-eons away. The ocean was full.

A blue-green haze swallowed everything around me. It took all that I had to stay calm. Less than a meter away, Belen faded into the murk until the shadow of her shadow was all that remained. The boat above us disappeared and then there was nothing. Nothing above; nothing below. Nothing but blue-green.

We descended further, the water getting darker as well as cloudier until I couldn't see my hands, my breathing getting shallower and faster until, as if by magic, the water cleared. There was a line, turbid above, clear beneath. The lower edge of a vast, undersea cloud.

A little further still and the open, empty darkness was not quite so empty. Something was there in the black; the cable, dark and thicker than I could wrap my arms around. It stretched as far as I could see in either direction. All along its length hung the socks, tall, mesh cylinders bulging with fist-sized mussels.

One after another, we harvested and replaced. Belen showed me how to attach the hook of the crane to the loop of a sock, and how to signal to Captain Haru it was ready to be lifted. Then we waited as the sock ascended, pulled up into the undersea cloud. I could imagine, just as easily, that it fell—plummeting into the thick atmosphere of some gassy moon I was orbiting. In the dark, open depths, there was no up or down; I was weightless. Belen had been right, I loved it.

When the replacement sock came, she showed me how to guide it gently to the cable. Since it was mostly empty, with just a smattering of mussel seed, it was easy to pull around. We lined the ends up so that one draped over each side of the cable. Belen let me unhook the crane and connect it to the next sock.

As I floated, waiting, I imagined I was Yuri outside his spaceship for the first time. I exhaled, and the bubbles streamed up from somewhere near the back of my helmet. I watch them dancing their way to the surface, imagining they were stars.

That was all it took. A moment of distraction.

It was just a light bump as I drifted past one of the dangling socks. Something caught. A valve on my tank, or a clasp on my wetsuit. I couldn't swim away. I couldn't turn. I couldn't move.

In that moment I realized just how very, very far I was below the ocean's surface. Underwater, I couldn't have called to Belen if I had thought to, but I didn't think. *If you know what you have to do* ... fighting panic, I put my feet against the sock ... *it is better not to look* ... I kicked off as hard as I could. The only way to get free. Something shifted inside the sock, and for a moment I moved forward. Then it pulled back twice as hard.

I wheezed. The full weight of the sock and all its mussels slammed against me, knocking the air from my lungs. I coughed, trying to find my wind. I coughed on water.

Water!

I hadn't heard my helmet crack, but water was seeping in. A slow, cold trickle. I moved my head. A stream of bubbles ran towards the surface. Water flooded past my chin. There was nothing I could do. My arms flailed. My legs kicked. I tried to lift my head; anything to keep my mouth above the water. It surged past my ears. I gasped and choked on salt.

A firm hand grabbed my shoulder. Belen! I grabbed back and pulled, together we could … she kicked me, hard. What little air I had left bubbled out of my nose.

Another blow. Belen pinned me with her bodyweight, holding me down. Drowning me. I tried to fight. Tried to push off her. Then, in one, firm motion, she grabbed my helmet and twisted. The water stopped seeping in. Only the seal had broken. She held me as, with the regulator, she purged air back into the helmet. She continued to hold me until I stopped struggling, until my breathing returned to normal. Until I was calm.

With her hand on mine, Belen guided my hand to the single loop of netting that had tangled around a valve of my air tank. She made me work it free from the sock. Then we ascended together slowly, her guiding me firmly the whole way to the top.

"You panicked," Belen said back at the surface, back on the *Buena Mañana.*

"I— I was drowning."

"Divers get tangled. Helmets come loose. But, if you had stayed calm …" she frowned. "It's panic that kills, down here and up above."

I wanted to cry.

"You're learning," she said, more gently. "Next time you'll do better."

"N— Next time?" I was shivering, even though I wasn't cold.

Belen wrapped her arm around my shoulder. "Do you know why they want us up there—the orbital companies?" She wiped a tear from my cheek. "Truth is, you can't stow away without someone noticing. We'd never even make it onto the crawler of a research ship, but the mining ships, they want us. Not because we'll work hard, because we're disposable. Everything up there is dangerous. They only *hire* people for the safest jobs. A stowaway gets drilled through by a micrometeorite, there is no paperwork. Construction is better than mining. More jobs to transition to inside. But we only get promoted if, when we fall, we get back up."

I dove more times that day because Belen made me, and over the next few because there was work to do, and I wanted to. I never had another problem, but the thought was always there in the back of my head: it only takes one mistake. If I had stayed calm, if I hadn't panicked ... I thought of my fearless mother, and for perhaps the second time in my life I wondered, what if I wasn't meant for space? Maybe I took after my father. Maybe Space Sickness ran in my blood.

When the night sky was clear, Belen and Captain Haru liked to sit out on the roof of the *Buena Mañana* and watch the stars. I lay beside them as we rocked gently in the ocean waves, not a light between us and the horizon. This, at least, was somewhere I belonged. To look, at least, the stars were free.

"When the first explorers sailed across the equator," Belen said, "they found different constellations in a different sky and had to write new stories to make sense of them. It will be the same up in space. When we finally leave the solar system the stars in the sky will move. We will say things like 'Orion is getting fat, we must be moving towards Betelgeuse', or 'Aquarius has sprung a leak, adjust to starboard'."

"I think they will have computers to tell them where to go," I said. Computers with future engineers like José to program them.

"Computers only say what someone told them to say. I will want to know for myself what I am looking at." Belen said.

"Then look," said Haru. "What a view we have from here." He had been silent so long, I hadn't realized he was listening.

"They need us up there," Belen said, "Space will be tamed by its workers, not its astronauts. For every Magellan or Columbus, there were a hundred unnamed sailors—every bit as impressive—just less well known."

"You are already an important part of it." Haru said. "Until someone finds mussels growing on asteroids, they need you here."

"They will, though," said Belen. "Not mussels, but something. They will forget us eventually. Everyone says there is nothing up there to support life, but that is the same way we used to think of the ocean. When the Polynesians first packed their whole families on boats, they set sail without knowing what they would find. For them the ocean was as hostile as space is to our explorers today."

"Space is not an ocean," Haru said.

"Most of the ocean is empty and inhospitable," Belen said, "but those early explorers found ways of telling what was over the horizon to find islands they needed, and ways of telling what was below the waves to find the fish. We will too. They looked for clouds to find islands with freshwater springs; we will use spectroscopy to tell if asteroids have water and oxides to harvest."

"Maybe someday," Haru said, "but not yet."

"Someday," Belen echoed a little more somberly. She, like me, was looking at the elevator—that glowing purple line—and not the stars behind it.

Belen saw it first.

I know because of the way she swore under her breath and shifted in her seat. In hindsight, that was to block my view. I thought she had cut her hand on a mussel, as I had already a half dozen times that morning. Between the waves and the sweeping shadow of a turbine blade, it could have been anything floating out there.

Haru was not so discreet. "*Puta!*" he swore and jumped to his feet.

"Just leave it," Belen tried. "It's already dead."

There was a sinking feeling in my gut.

"Him, not it," Haru said tersely, "*he* will spoil the waters."

By the time Haru returned with a boathook, *he* had drifted close, bumping against the hull of the *Buena Mañana* with each wave; a human body floating in the water.

His eyes were open, staring up at the sky as what remained of his clothes billowed gently in the waves. The skin was bleached of all color, but with that dark, matted hair and those emaciated cheeks he could only have come from Manta.

"Laika," Belen said urgently. "Go grab a tarp."

"No, we need her help first." Haru hooked under the torso with his pole.

"He'll cook in this sun," Belen insisted. She was already half over the side, grabbing at an arm.

"This is not the last corpse she will see out here. She will need to toughen up eventually."

When I did not leave, Belen relented. "Grab a leg."

The stench was unbearable even before we pulled him from the water. As the body flopped onto the deck with the unpleasant sound of a wet sponge hitting wood, seawater and built-up gasses began to gurgle from his throat. I didn't gag—but Belen did.

Haru walked off to grab the tarp himself. Once again, I could not make myself move.

"If *he* couldn't be bothered to figure out the ocean," Belen told me after Haru had left, "I don't know how *he* expected to figure out space."

I did not help them wrap the body. All I could do was stare. I kept thinking, *He is just a boy. Maybe thirteen or fourteen, my age or younger.* I had not expected that.

I had always known there would be bodies around the elevator, everyone did. *They litter the sea.* But when I had imagined dead bodies floating in the ocean, they were always old. It made no sense, I know. Octogenarians did not try to stow away, but dead and old just went together. At least, they had until then.

I felt sick. I don't remember if I made it to the side of the boat before I threw up.

The dead boy needed glasses—when he was alive, that is. There were small divots in the sides of his head, just above his ears, the kind people got from wearing too-small glasses all their life. When he was young, and did not yet have those glasses, I bet he couldn't see the elevator —even when the light was just right. What about the mansions on the hill? If he could, he looked up there and said, like everyone did when they were too young to know better, "One day I will own one of those." Only, the mansions on the hill grew larger, not more numerous.

Manta used to have factories, and I decided that the dead boy's mother worked in one of those. Maybe a factory making space helmets for the astronauts who went up. She even took one home as a souvenir. She set it on a shelf in the starter home she bought on the side of the valley—back when she could afford a starter home and glasses. Back before the factories closed, there were many people like that.

They were already building spaceships in orbit before the elevator was finished, but they were not building helmets there. Not until someone who already had a mansion on the top of a hill realized it was cheaper to send up tightly packed ingots of metal and solid glass than large, empty helmets. I bet that someone bought their neighbor's mansion after thinking up that idea, so they could tear it down and make their own bigger.

The new space helmets were 3D-printed in a workshop at the top of the elevator, and the factories down in Manta were boarded up. After that, things got harder for everyone, except those who owned the elevator or the workshops up in space. The dead boy's mother had to sell her home and did not buy a new one. She should have sold her souvenir helmet too. Maybe then it wouldn't have been so tempting for her son.

Sometimes my mother did not eat so she could keep me fed, and we were better off than most in the valley. I wondered what it had been like for the boy. Had he waited at the docks like I did, hoping the next boat might pick him instead of someone else? Maybe he had tried to work, and stood in line outside one of the few factories left, hoping it would let him in before it closed too. I could not tell from his bloated hands if he had ever tried another way, or if the elevator was his first as well as his last idea. I would never know if he was like me, drawn to a dream, or if he just had nowhere else to turn but up.

People like us would never get factory jobs or starter homes. People like us made our own way or starved. But if even Yuri had floated away, what hope did the rest of us have?

Belen disappeared, leaving Haru and I to pull the rest of the mussels from the socks. He worked quickly, making up for lost time. I was next to useless. My hands would not stop shaking.

When I couldn't take the silence anymore, I asked, "Do they ever make it—the people who try to ride the elevator?"

He looked at me a moment, then out to sea, as though contemplating the question very carefully. The whole time, his hands never stopped sorting. "Have you made it, Laika?" He finally asked.

"I'm trying," I said.

Haru nodded. "Me too." Then he added, seeing my confused look, "*Make it* is a relative term. The Buddha preaches contentment. If one is content with what they have, then they have *made it*. If one always wants more, then it does not matter how much they have. Those who climb, some of them will *make it* up the elevator, but then what? Have they *made it*? They will share a bunk with five others and work more hours than there are in a day. How long do you really think they will last? A month? A season? Of those who *make it* that far, and that's pretty far, most will be dead within a year. But will they have *made it*? A year with a bunk and two meals a day would be *making it* for some of the people I have seen floating out here."

Haru shook his head. "We tell stories because they give us hope. We say that if someone can make it up the elevator, if they can work hard and stay safe, if they have just the right luck, if they get noticed by just the right people, then maybe they can *make it*—whatever that means. And of course, we say, if they can do it, we could too—if we had to, not that we will. There is a certain comfort to that, no?"

"I don't know." It did not seem comforting.

"You come from Manta. Tell me, have you heard about the mansion that is owned by a former stowaway?"

I nodded. "Everyone has."

"If we were closer to the shore," Haru asked, "could you point it out for me?"

I shook my head. The closest I had ever been was when a *mudak* who liked my mother decided to take us both for a drive in his car. Even he, in his fancy car, couldn't get through the community gates.

"I have heard many stories about starship captains who were once stowaways until they worked their way up. They always retire with a mansion of their own. I've heard it a thousand times, but if even a tenth of those stories were true, then almost all of the mansions on Manta's hill must belong to former stowaways by now. I'd think, if that were the case, then you, a local, could point out one or two for sure. *Apocryphal*, that is what we call stories like that.

"The Buddha preaches contentment. That should be easy for us. You'd think fully bellies, a roof to lay on, and a part to play in what we watch going on above would be enough. We do have a part, Laika, all of us, however small. We feed Manta; without Manta, no elevator, no space. But still, we long for more. We dream dreams and say someday it will be us who *make it*, because there is no real harm in that, until there is.

"Truth is, that boy on the deck never had a chance; maybe thinking he did is what kept him going on hungry nights, but it is also what made him think he could make it up the elevator. I'm sure that even the Buddha looked forward to a dry fire when it rained, but he knew the difference between a dream and reality. That the boy died in the end, that is tragic —but maybe he lived first because of his dream. That, in a way, would have been *making it*—would it not? If only he had known when a dream should remain just a dream."

Belen was at the back of the boat leaning against a railing, looking out towards the elevator as though nothing had happened.

We were close enough now that the crawlers had taken form. The colorful squiggles of company logos were almost clear enough to read—perhaps if I knew their designs better. Belen did not look at me as I approached, but her hand wiped something from her cheek.

She took a sharp, deep breath. "It gets easier," she said, but she did not sound like she believed it. "Just know, for every floater we find out here, there are ten stowaways who make it to the top."

Holding On, by Justen Russell

That didn't sound right, but neither did arguing.

"Would you have tried swimming?" Belen asked. "Out on the dock, if I hadn't picked you?" She turned with red ringed-eyes. I had never seen her like that. "If I had picked the fat man instead of you. How long would you have waited for another boat before trying on your own?"

The elevator was too far to swim, but with a raft—would I have tried that eventually? Would I have ended up just like the boy under the tarp? "I don't know," I said. "It's a good thing you chose me."

"Is it?" Belen asked. "I always say I'm going to go up there someday, and Haru laughs with me. Like it's a joke we are sharing, like it's a game. But it's not. Not to me. I want to ride the elevator, Laika. I want to be in space, I ..." She shook her head. "I keep pretending that I can. I keep saying, 'soon'. That I am almost ready, that I have it almost planned out, that I have to be smart about it.

"I *have* planned it, Laika, you know I have planned it all and planned it all again, but there is only so long I can keep planning and keep pretending that it will happen.

"Every time we are near the elevator, I look at the logos on the crawlers and I actually hope it says NASA, because then I will have an excuse. Then, at least, I can live with myself when I don't. They don't like stowaways on research vessels.

"Twice now it has been for a mining firm, and I didn't go. I could have. There was a pressurized crate and I could have just snuck inside. You know I know how. Maybe they would have caught me. Maybe they would have sent me back down. Maybe it wouldn't have resealed, and I would have died on the way up, but I will never know because I didn't even try."

"I'm glad you didn't die." I wasn't sure what else to say.

"I wish I were dying," Belen said. "How sick is that? I wish I were starving. I tell myself that if I were starving, that if I had no other choice, that if I would die if I didn't find a way to stowaway on the next crawler, I would risk it. I would try because I would have nothing left to lose … but that's not true. I will always have a reason to wait. What does that mean, Laika, that even in my dreams I only go out of desperation, only because there was no other way?"

"That you have something to lose," I said. "That's not such a bad thing."

"Is it?" Belen snapped. "I'm what—too lucky?—too fortunate? Too rich to be desperate enough to follow my dreams— yet too poor for there to be another way." She laughed. Not a happy laugh, an unpleasant half a snort, half a sob. "I'm jealous of a corpse, Laika. It's ridiculous. I am being ridiculous. He is dead. He was stupid and now he is dead and under a tarp and still, I want to be him because at least he tried. At least he had the chance to get lucky. At least he got to know. How pathetic is that? How can that make any sense?"

I never really knew the right words to say. That was my mother. I never had her smile. I pulled Belen close for a hug.

"I want to go," she said, "even if it doesn't work out. Even if I end up dead. I just want to know. Was I good enough? Could I have made it? I want to be up there right now looking down on this ocean of *merda*." She sunk into my arms. "Why can't I do that?"

I spoke my mother's words: "When you know what you have to do, it is better not to look. Just go."

"If only it were that easy," Belen said. "I don't know if I am more scared that I will fall, or that I will never even try—but I'm scared, Laika. I'm scared."

"I'm scared too." I said, and I was. As they never used to tire of telling me: the real Laika, the Russian dog, she died on the way up.

"You're just a kid," Belen said. "You still have time." Did I? Or had we both already looked over the edge and seen the rocks below.

In the morning, as the sun shone from the east, I could see the elevator. Not one thread, but several—six parallel lines stretched taut between the sky and a metal island in the middle of the ocean. I made up my mind before we were close enough to read the labels on the crawlers —if they were wrong, I would wait on that island until they were right. When you know what you have to do, it is better not to look.

I laid my equipment out along the deck —like Belen had for diving—and chose from the regulators hidden in the back of the locker. Those designed for altitude, not diving. Belen had planned everything, and then planned again.

I felt a pang of guilt as I set a helmet on the deck, but there wasn't time for that. I would be forgiven; this was why she had brought me here, to show her it was possible. I took one slow, calming breath, then changed my mind. I ran down the stairs into the *Buena Mañana*'s cabin to where Belen was still asleep.

"I'm going," I whispered, nudging Belen awake. "Come with me. Don't think, just come." She didn't understand but sat up, too groggy to resist my pull, at least, at first.

We were halfway up the stairs when she asked about Haru. I shook my head and pulled her harder. There was no time to slow down.

"He'll be fine." He had his contentment. There were plenty of others in Manta who would love to harvest mussels and look up at the stars. "This is the reason you chose me, isn't it?" The big man on the dock would never have pulled Belen up with him, would never have thought to look up at all.

"Objectif." Belen gasped as we stepped into the sun, and I looked—though I shouldn't have, because I truly did not want to know. The colorful squiggles on one crawler's glossy sides had resolved into the square and circle logo of Objectif Outre-Terre—an orbital construction company.

"We have to go now," I said.

I pulled Belen to the equipment and helped her put it on. Gear for the swim to the island, and gear to stay warm on the ride up.

"I can't," she said, then, as I tried to put a helmet on her head, she finally stopped me. "What if …"

"We could die," I agreed, "maybe. Or we could live. Don't you want to know?" The sea may be littered with the bodies of those who did not *make it*, but Manta was choked full of those who never even tried.

"I want to try," I said. Reflected in Belen's helmet, the elevator did not seem so tall. It seemed to bend towards us— bowing. No one kept statistics on stowaways, but I doubt half made it as far as we already had. "Don't think," I said, "jump."

She let me put the helmet on her head.

With it on, Belen could have been Mimi. It was my own reflection, however, that caught me off guard. Even missing three teeth, I had Yuri's smile: bright, infectious, *content.* We were going to space. The mutts were going to fly.

"Hold on," I said, as I took her hand and we jumped.

See Justen Russell's story "Holding On" online at Metaphorosis.
If you liked it, leave a comment. Authors love that!
Remember to subscribe to our e-mail updates so you'll know when new stories are posted.

About the story

At its core, "Holding On" is about coming to terms with what it means to follow your dreams. In our world, very few people will ever be astronauts, or presidents, or best-selling authors. Even among the privileged and connected, who have more opportunities than most, luck can be more important than skill. In the face of abysmal odds, as we grow up, most of us will replace our childhood dreams with the more attainable sort.

I don't think I ever acknowledged giving up on certain dreams. Somewhere between middle school and University I simply relegated the moonshot goals from "someday soon" to "someday." Very purposely, I never pursued them. Despite wanting to write, it was safer to leave it as a dream for the future, "when I had something to say." The reality was, in putting words to the page I would have had to confront the very real risk that I might fail.

The idea for "Holding On" was flushed out during the first lockdown of the COVID-19 pandemic. In Paris, where I was living, we were mostly confined to our homes. One hour of outdoor activity was permitted each day, provided we were alone and stayed within one kilometer of our apartments. Surrounded by tall buildings, there were only a few spaces I could stand to feel the sun on my skin. It was in one of those, looking up at the bright blue sky, that I started to wonder what a space elevator would look like. Would it seem to taper, would it be visible from a distance, would it seem to curve towards a vanishing point in the sky? Europe has no shortage of tall, impressive monuments. There are architectural spaces that play with space to invoke a sense of grandeur. I have stood beneath building meant to humble me and felt incredibly small. I could imagine what a space elevator would feel like to look at, but not what I would actually see. Maybe that is why I kept coming back to it?

Laika, Belen, and Haru all grew out of those imaginings. I could feel what it would be like for them, growing up, working and living in the shadows of a gateway to the stars. What would it be like to have, always on the horizon, a constant reminder of how small your life currently is, and how big it could be. Living in an impressive city of my own, with great monuments visible along the horizon, far outside of my one-kilometer existence, I could empathize at least a little with their plight.

The mussels came from an article I read about mussel farming off deep-sea wind turbines in the Netherlands. Floating away in space was a deep-seated fear of my wife's that she wanted me to share. The parallels between Polynesian- and space-exploration—that is a pet comparison of mine. I think there are many parallels in the past to the transformations of today: space exploration, artificial intelligence, genetic engineering, migration, inequality, even if the specifics are different.

I suppose you could say "Holding On" came from having far too much time to think and far too little to do but dream my own dreams and turn "someday" back into "someday soon." A big thank you to all those who helped me flesh this story out.

A question for the author

Q: Do you live near where you were born? Have you traveled much?

A: While not quite antipodal, France is an ocean and the bulk of a continent away from my hometown in Western Canada. I suppose you could say that is far away—my parents certainly would. The more I travel, however, and the more places I live, the more "near" becomes a relative term.

I spent a lot of my childhood wrapped up in the casual regionalism that a child uses to define who they are. To be Calgarian (my hometown) was to be not

Edmontonian (our rival town), then I moved further and learned I was Albertan (the province of both cities). To be Canadian was to be not American. Then I moved to Europe and learned I was North American all along.

Of course, I changed too. I never feel more North American than when I am outside of the continent, and less North American than when I return to visit.

I have lived in eight cities across two continents, and intend to live in many more. I am excited to see how my worldview shifts with wherever I reside next.

I travel a lot, too. As much as I can. Mostly locally (local to wherever I am living at the time) but sometimes further afield. I feel like "being a tourist" is a skill, and one that I am getting better at with each voyage. I've learned what it is that I like to experience and see when I travel. There are a lot of tourist traps in the world, but sometimes tourist hotspots are must-sees for a reason. If you are ever in Istanbul, you should go and see the Hagia Sophia—it is absolutely amazing—but my core memories of Istanbul are from leaving the beaten path, getting lost, and getting to know the locals.

Of course, if you do travel, it is important to be respectful. Tourism can be damaging to a culture and a place. Especially when we treat someone else's home as a commodity we are entitled to 'because we paid'. When done right, however, travel is not just incredibly rewarding but also incredibly important. We need to meet people who think differently from ourselves, and experience different ways of living. A little cross-cultural awareness can go a long way towards solving many of the important problems of our world.

So, do I think of France as far from where I was born? No, not anymore. I did at first, when I first arrived and didn't speak the language. When I didn't know anyone and I just wanted to go back home. Now that I have gotten to know the people and learned to think a little more like a local, France is home. I wonder where home will be next.

About the author

Justen Russell is a scientist and author, with a PhD in the biological sciences. He lives in Paris, France with his partner and their child. He is anachronistic in his athletics, enjoying historical sword-fighting and swing dance

www.justenrussell.com

Infinite Possibilities II

Michael Gardner

Adrian receives a USB drive in the mail that has footage of a cabin, nothing else. His wife, Candice, thinking it a game, encourages him to solve the mystery. It's apparent that Adrian and Candice's relationship is strained, especially since Candice's mother died.

Adrian stumbles across the location of the cabin and agrees to explore it with Candice. Inside, they find a television, a recliner, a book. The television switches on and reveals a man that looks like Adrian. Other Adrian. The television shuts down before Candice notices. But Candice discovers something else. The book—*Infinite Possibilities: Navigating the Multiverse*—is apparently written by Adrian.

2

He reads at his work bench in the garage. His tools are neatly packed away, and he's wiped the surface down, but it carries the familiar scent of oil and grease. That scent comforts him, grounds him, as he tries to make sense of the book from the cabin. The book with his name on the front.

The multiverse gives life to all possibilities simultaneously. Within it we find infinite, parallel worlds. The fundamentals of these worlds may differ markedly from our own, barely at all, or in some cases, replicate our own world almost exactly.

As I write these words, there is another version of me doing the same thing in their world. And another version of me doing something different, perhaps mowing the lawn while the weather remains warm. There also exist versions of me profoundly different: someone that communicates telepathically, someone that exists in a non-physical state, someone with abilities I can't even fathom. In yet other worlds, I do not exist at all.

Adrian stops, closes his eyes and rubs them with his knuckles. The pressure brings flashes of light into the darkness behind his lids, like lightning streaking across a clouded night sky. Something about the writing, the certainty of it is jarring.

He opens his eyes, turns a couple of pages, picks a passage at random.

Identification and observation has shown us much, but to truly advance discovery, we need to make contact with other worlds, and then determine the means to traverse them. While some in my profession have argued that this latter step cannot be supported by the laws of physics and mathematics, I would remind them that the multiverse contains all possibilities, including that other worlds are governed by laws different to our own. These worlds may already possess the technology to move from one world to the next. It may be as simple as opening a door and stepping through.

As such, I would posit that discovering the means to move between worlds is not a question of how, but when. In the meantime, while we wait for the people with the means to find us, we must focus on advances within our power to make. We must meet them halfway.

The garage door begins to rise, breaking Adrian's focus. He stretches his neck, turns to find Candice ducking under the door. Her car is parked out front, as usual. She's carrying a plastic bag.

"You want to take a break for lunch?" she says, raising the bags. He can see the outline of takeaway containers through the plastic. He suddenly realises how hungry he is.

"Lunch?" he says. "Already?" She glides toward him like she's floating across the garage. She stops next to Adrian, places a hand on his shoulder. A casual gesture. A gesture Adrian is beginning to enjoy again.

"Yes, it's after one and I'm starving. I thought you might be too, so I grabbed some Thai. You interested?"

He glances at the open book, then back at Candice. Nods. "Sure," he says. "That sounds nice."

"So, anything interesting? Any clues about what we do next?"

He shakes his head. "No, not yet."

"May I?" she asks, motioning to the book.

He shrugs, and she takes that as agreement. She starts to turn pages with her free hand, rifling them roughly. It makes him wince, but he doesn't say anything. He doesn't like the idea of pages tearing, which he keeps expecting as she flips them so quickly. He can see she's not really reading, just searching for something to stand out. A signpost that says: 'go here next'. But he's less and less convinced that that is what this is. What it is instead, he doesn't know.

He jumps when Candice slaps the book with her open hand. The sound reverberates around the garage. She grins. "What about this?"

He looks at the pages she's found. Schematics. A plan for some kind of electronic device. He hunches closer, studies it. He turns the page and finds further instructions. He goes back, looks at the materials required.

"Well?" she says.

"Well what?"

"You build things. The book has your name on it. Seems like the next step in the game, doesn't it?"

He builds things, he repeats to himself. It suddenly seems hot in the garage. He can feel the blood pulsing in his temples.

The next step for someone like him. He studies the diagram again and what strikes him as odd is its relative simplicity. Surely, in a book about complex physics, schematics should also be complex. They shouldn't be understood by bus drivers who like to tinker with lawn mowers. And yet he does understand. Or enough of it to think he could start building, and perhaps fill in any gaps in his knowledge with YouTube. Candice is right, this appears to be made for him.

"Maybe," he says. He closes the book abruptly, stands. His eyes dart to Candice who frowns, but she doesn't say anything. Not yet anyway.

"We don't want to let the food get cold, do we?" he says, forcing a smile. Her frown deepens. "I'll come back to this later," he tries.

She pauses a beat. "Okay," she says. She gives him one last uncertain look, then turns and makes her way into the house.

He doesn't follow straight away. He casts an eye toward the book again. Just seeing it lying on his bench is unsettling. The book, the USB, the cabin, what he may or may not have seen on that TV screen—together they create a cocktail of uneasiness that he suspects might go away if he just let it all be. Yet, as he stares, he realises he'll come back to it, and construct whatever it is he's meant to construct.

He tells himself it's because Candice won't let up. But the truth is something else. It's him. He needs to know where this leads.

Not long after he proposed, Candice told him she wanted to elope.

They were in a public park, lying on a picnic blanket, the sky clear and bright overhead. They'd brought a bottle of wine and some cheese in a picnic basket. The park was mostly green lawns dotted with a few large trees. It was sparsely populated—only a few families chasing kids or giving the dogs a run. From a playground in the distance came the sounds of childish laughter and squeals of delight.

"Why?" he asked.

She shrugged, rolled onto her back, stared up at the sky. He smiled as he watched her. She was beautiful. He found everything about her confident, nonchalant attitude striking.

"You love me, I love you. I couldn't give a shit about all of the phony hangers-on."

"Our parents?"

She made a dismissive 'psst' sound, glanced at him sideways. "As bad as the rest. They're not in it for us. It's about them. Status with their friends, or plain old pride. I don't want to do something for others. I want to do it for us."

"Where?"

"I don't know. Fiji, maybe? Hawaii? God, we could go to the middle of Australia for all I care, if it's just us."

She rolled back onto her side, faced him, reached out and cupped his jaw in her hand. "This is about us, right?

He leaned toward her, kissed her. Her lips were soft. He pulled away, exhaled a long time.

"Of course," he said. "Yes, of course. I'll marry you wherever you want. Alone on a beach, in a small country pub, wherever. I love you."

She smiled. Kissed him again. "I knew my adventurous Adrian was still in there somewhere."

"Always," he whispered.

She smiled like she didn't believe him. He felt a pang of hurt but didn't say anything. Part of him knew she was right. He wasn't the same as he had been. And yet who was? People grew up, right? One of them had to level out. And if he hadn't, he and Candice would likely have fed off each other, added rocket fuel to rocket fuel, exploded.

They married twelve months later, in a church, in front of family and friends. It was a cliché, but it was the happiest day of his life. He knew Candice had only just tolerated it. Had done it for him, which he'd appreciated at the time.

Yet after, he noticed a subtle change in her. Like she'd realised that he wasn't who he purported to be. Like he'd broken a promise. Not just about the wedding, but about who he was.

Adrian shuts the welder off, flips his visor up. His work is rough, but he can see the joins will hold.

He's created a metal cube: one foot, by one foot, by one foot. The top plate is set with hinges so he can access the interior. There are two holes in the casing: one for the antenna, one for the control panel, both to be attached later. The instructions tell him that the machine will be powered by an internal battery. Convenient, he thinks, for operation anywhere, including at the cabin. He's not sure why that thought pops into his head. He has no reason to think he needs to return there again. Yet that is what he thinks.

He's hot in his coveralls. There're large sweat patches under each arm, and sweat is beaded in his hairline where the welding helmet sits. The garage door is wide open, and a gentle breeze pushes hot air around. The scent of ozone and heated metal permeates the air. He removes his helmet and tosses it onto the bench with a thud.

He found the materials for the casing at his local hardware store, but he ordered the electronic components online. Most should arrive in a week or so, although the motherboard and power supply unit are coming from overseas, so they'll take longer.

He wonders what this thing is for, and what it will do if it works. The book is not at all clear on the machine's purpose. It descends into indecipherable jargon that, no matter how many times Adrian has read it, obscures clear meaning and insight. Perhaps it will do nothing. Perhaps something confounding. Adrian has the unrealistic expectation that he will discover its purpose as he continues to piece it together.

The next step is to create the internal frame for the electronics. He has everything ready, and it shouldn't take long for him to construct, yet his eyes feel sore, gritty. When he holds a hand up level with his face, he sees a slight tremor. He's been at this longer than he can recall. He removes a welding glove, checks his watch, and is not entirely surprised to find it's nearly four.

He doesn't want to stop, but he knows he must. Candice doesn't know he skipped work to do this. Even though she wants him to build the machine, he knows she won't approve of him giving up another shift.

He takes one last look at his work, then begins to tidy his materials away.

Even after they were married, he continued the fantasy that bus driving was temporary, because that seemed important to Candice. To her vision of him, and what he could be. Like most secrets bottled up, it came out at the wrong time, hurt them both.

They were having drinks with a couple from Candice's accounting firm—Dan and Gillian. It was a Friday night, and Candice had booked a table at a new bar in the city. They were tucked away at the back of the venue, but they still had to raise their voices to hear each other over the thrum of the music and the crowd.

Gillian seemed pleasant enough, but Dan rubbed Adrian the wrong way. Dan's eyes lingered on Candice, only to slide away when an attractive woman passed their table on the way to the bar. Dan didn't even try to hide his lurid gaze from Gillian, who seemed happy to ignore it.

"What do you do, Adrian?" Dan directed at him, before his gaze moved back to the crowd. It was an inevitable question, but when Dan asked it, Adrian felt Candice bristle beside him.

"I drive buses," he answered, took a sip from his beer, placed it back on the table with a clink. Dan looked back, cocked an eyebrow, and at the corners of his mouth, a smirk.

"Really. How fascinating. Good honest job, eh?" It was said with condescension, but Adrian chose to ignore it.

"Suits me fine."

Which should have been the end of it, except Candice jumped in. "He's going back to university next semester. He's going to study law, right, Adrian? Tell him."

Adrian grimaced, tried not to show his annoyance. Candice didn't seem to notice. She stared at Dan as Dan watched Adrian. Before he could say anything, Dan spoke.

"The law. Now that's an interesting field of study. Plenty of good jobs in law when you're done, and not just as a lawyer. We have a bunch of good people with a law background in our firm, believe it or not."

Candice agreed, started offering a few of her own thoughts on the benefits of a law degree. Adrian had heard it all before. It shouldn't have irked him as much as it did. But it did. In part it was Dan. The guy was a jerk. But he hated that Candice was so eager to please that arsehole. And perhaps worse, that she seemed ashamed of Adrian.

The words spilled out before he could stop them.

"I hate lawyers. And I fucking hate the way people with a degree look down on those without one, like the feudal system still exists and they've just been made a Lord," he said. His outburst brought an abrupt end to Dan and Candice's discussion. Gillian and Dan both turned to look at him strangely, Candice's face frozen in shock.

"I'm sorry, babe. But I like my job. I don't want," he motioned toward Dan, "to be like that." Dan straightened in his seat, glared at Adrian through narrowed eyes. He looked like he was about to say something spiteful, but Gillian took his arm and squeezed gently. He closed his mouth, remained quiet.

"Let's not do this here," Candice said, and shot an awkward smile across the table toward Dan and Gillian. Adrian ignored her.

"Look, I haven't enrolled in university. I know I said I would, but..." he sighed. "I've made up my mind. I just hadn't got around to telling you."

"You what?" she hissed at him, her mouth a thin, angry line.

"Didn't seem to me it really affected you. Unless you can only love me if I become a corporate crony."

"Oh, fuck you," she said.

Gillian coughed, suggested to Dan that they go get another drink from the bar.

"No need," Adrian said as he pushed his chair back and stood. "Time for me to get to bed. I have a big day tomorrow. You know, driving the bus."

He walked out before anyone could stop him.

The truth was he was pissed at Candice. And himself.

He had enjoyed physics when they first met, had done a few undergraduate courses in astrophysics, was thinking seriously about majoring in it. Candice had thought that too niche, too likely to end with a career in academia. Something Adrian had thought sounded okay, but Candice had grander plans. She convinced him he needed to pursue study that led to a job that paid well. That had options for career advancement. At that time, all he wanted to do was impress her, so he tried it her way.

But nothing stuck. He enrolled in the courses she suggested. Tried them and failed them. Hated them. Instead of leading to a career with money at the end, it led to the accumulation of student debt.

He took the bus driving job mostly to avoid studying. He found he liked it. The familiar routes, the resonant drone of the engine, it put him in a relaxed state, helped him think. What he thought was that if he'd done things his way, he might have been happier.

So, without telling Candice, he re enrolled in physics. He was excited when he walked into his first class, but from that first day he realised something was wrong. Something had passed him by. Like his brain had changed with age. He found the lectures incredibly difficult. Yet the kids that surrounded him didn't seem to share his confusion. He felt old, stupid. He wasn't. He understood machines, could pull apart an engine with his eyes closed. That was something, at least. Not the same, but something.

When he dropped out, he knew with a gut punch finality that university was no longer an option. He felt a failure. And he knew he would cop Candice's judgement when he told her. Perhaps that's why he told Candice the way he did. Maybe her anger was better than her pity.

They fought when Candice got home. Fought as hard as they had since they'd married. They made up a few days later anyway, but things changed. Candice talked less and less about her job, about office politics, about annoying clients. She still invited Adrian to drinks with friends and colleagues from time to-time, but Adrian declined more readily, and Candice seemed happy to accept that.

He initially thought the confrontation had been good for them. Helped set some boundaries. But in time he found that being separated from such a large part of Candice's life began to feel as if he were floating in one bubble, and Candice another.

"Oh," Candice says with a start when she walks into the kitchen. She raises a hand to her chest, stops.

Adrian's sitting at the bench, drinking a glass of water. He feels fresh, clean, his hair still wet from his shower.

"I thought you'd still be at work?" she says, appraising him with curiosity.

"Just a short shift today," he lies, keeps his face neutral. She used the front door for once, so he knows she hasn't seen the machine casing. He's both pleased and disappointed.

Candice finally moves again, tosses the mail onto the bench.

"How was your day?" he asks, perfunctorily. He picks up the envelopes, rifles through them.

"Busy." She drops her handbag onto the floor near the fridge, sighs. "But it's good to be finished, and not have to think about work for a couple of days."

He looks at her confused, then realises it's Friday. He forgets sometimes, working shifts. The days tend to blur.

"I was going to head out with Jenny and the girls tonight. I think some of the husbands are coming along. Do you want to join us?"

He shakes his head. "No, I'm good."

She doesn't look surprised, or disappointed. "Next time," she says, moving toward the back of the house.

He refocusses on the mail. Mostly bills. But then... another plain white envelope, his name typed in capital letters, a small bulge. He swallows.

"There's leftover quiche in the fridge," Candice calls out from their bedroom.

"Yeah, thanks," he says, distracted. He tears open the letter, upends it in his hand. Another USB.

His laptop is still where he left it on the bench. He grabs it, powers it up. From down the hall he hears a sliding door open, close. The shower starts to run. He can hear Candice humming over the patter of water.

He plugs in the USB, this time doesn't bother with antivirus or turning off the wifi; he just opens it and plays the video file.

At first it's just the hut again, standing alone amongst the canola, another sunny day. He knows it's not the same sunny day because there's a trail cut through the crop. It runs from the road up to the chain link fence, then around the perimeter toward the padlocked gate. The trail that he and Candice made.

The shot changes. It zooms out, slowly, until the hut appears to be a very long way away. It zooms until the road is prevalent. This is being filmed from the verge, he thinks. Maybe from someone's yard even, from one of the new houses. There's a distant drone, which rises in volume, like a symphony reaching a crescendo. A blur of white fills the screen. A blur that the camera follows until it resolves into the image of a bus. The number thirty-three. His bus. He wonders if he's driving it.

The bus doesn't slow. It eases around the gentle bend without braking, the sound changing pitch as it disappears from view.

The shot ends abruptly, is replaced with an image of an apartment building. It's about eight stories high, not new, but not old. Grey, unexciting architecture. An entrance at street level, glass doors, rows of silver mailboxes just inside, an elevator. The shot holds steady on that entrance. On the street, random people walk into shot, walk past the building entrance, walk out of shot. They crisscross like ants at work. Focussed.

Then Candice steps into frame. He recognises her instantly. She wears a navy pant suit, large beige handbag over her shoulder. Walking with her is a man he doesn't know. Tall, with dark curly hair. They walk in unison, not too close, not too far apart.

They veer toward the entrance of the apartment building, stop. He opens the door, holds it for her as she steps inside. They approach the elevators, she presses a button, they wait. When the doors open, they slip inside, turn, stand close at the back of the elevator. He thinks he sees a smile on her face as the doors close, but he can't be sure.

Then she's gone.

Adrian's stomach is a hard, tight knot. It feels uncomfortably full, like he's been chewing paper, swallowing it down until it's formed a wet, pulpy mass.

The video returns to the hut. An overcast day now. It looks like it could rain at any moment. It's a message, he thinks. An invitation to return.

"What's that, another video for your game?" Candice asks. He jerks upright, turns and sees her walking across the family room. Her head's cocked, her hands at her right ear fixing an earring.

He closes the laptop guiltily. Doesn't know why he should feel guilty. Nods. "Yep. Another USB."

"Can I look?" she says, finishing with her earring.

"No," he says more loudly than he intended. "There's nothing new. Just the hut again. The same video, really."

She stops by the dining table. "Really? That's odd."

"Maybe an error. I think the book's the thing to focus on."

She nods slowly. "Yeah. Sure. Well, let me know how you go? I won't be too late, okay?"

"Okay," he repeats.

She moves toward him, feathers his forehead with a fleeting kiss, grabs her handbag in a sweeping movement, then disappears toward the front of the house.

When he's certain she's gone, he opens the laptop and plays the video again.

They'd been married three years when he asked her about that night in Thailand.

They were renting at the time, an apartment in the city, close to her work. It was too expensive, and very small. The furniture was cheap—Ikea, gumtree seconds, that sort of thing. He was sitting on the couch rubbing his fingertips over the velvety material of the arm. He didn't recall buying the couch, or going with Candice to pick it up from someone's garage. So how did she get this back to the building, let alone up the three flights of stairs to their apartment?

She sat next to him, feet curled under her, watching a movie he recognised, but couldn't place. One with Tom Hanks in it. Something earnest. Weren't they all?

"Do you ever think about Mike?" he'd blurted out.

She turned slowly, looked at him in a way that suggested she'd just woken from a deep sleep. She cocked her head to the left. "Who?"

"Mike. That guy from Thailand. The couple we met and..." Like a car spluttering on an empty tank of fuel, he ran out of words.

She watched him for a moment, bemused. Then she smiled. Or was it a smirk? "Mike," she said, like she was tasting the word on her lips. "Mike. I must admit, I'd forgotten that was even his name."

She returned her attentions to the movie. For a second, he thought that might be it.

"I thought we agreed never to talk about it. That it was a one time thing?" she said, still staring ahead.

"It was," he jumped in quickly. "I mean, we did. I'm sorry. I don't know why I was thinking about it, it just... popped into my head.

"Do you think about her?" she asked, glancing at him. "What was her name again? I can't remember."

He grimaced. "Me neither."

And she laughed. A genuine laugh that rolled through her whole body. She grabbed the cushion from behind her back and hit him playfully with it. "You liar, it was Taylor."

He couldn't help but laugh too. He nodded. "Ah, yes. Now I remember."

She picked up the remote, muted the television, slid across the couch and wiggled her way under his arm. "What's up? Why are you asking about this after all this time?"

"I don't know," he said, as she rested her head on his chest.

"Do you regret it?" she asked.

"Do you?"

"I don't feel that strongly. It was something that happened."

"Oh," he said, squeezing her shoulder. "So… it was okay?"

She stifled a laugh. "Is that what's bugging you. How it was?" She placed her hand on his thigh. He swallowed, felt something stir. "Well, Mister, truth is, he was rubbish."

"Really," he said, his voice a rasp as she began to rub his leg, moving in circles, moving higher.

"Really," she whispered into his chest. "He had no idea what he was doing. So if I regret anything, it was that I wasted myself on him when I could have had the good stuff next door with you."

He smiled at that.

"What about you and Taylor. Was that okay?"

"Nah," he said quickly. "It was awkward as hell. I didn't feel comfortable at all. It was more like a chore then something to enjoy." Which was a lie, but he couldn't tell her the truth now. He wondered if she was lying as well.

"Good," she said. She undid the button on his pants, slipped her hand inside. "I don't know about you, but I think I've seen this movie. What about we go to bed, erase bad memories?"

As they made love, his thoughts strayed to his night with Taylor. When he came, the power of his orgasm surprised him. Just like back then.

He rolled aside, breathing heavily, wracked with guilt. Candice snuggled up close to him and he lay there, unable to say anything or move, still hoping Candice had lied to him earlier. But he had the feeling she hadn't. Which left him where, exactly?

The canola has a kind of bioluminescence under the waning moon. It's like wading through jellyfish. Adrian reaches the chain link fence, hooks his fingers through, squints, but the features of the cabin are unclear in the dark.

When he left the house, he initially decided to go to the city to find Candice. But he quickly realised he didn't know where to look for her. And what would he do if he did find her? Confront her? Probably not. Yet he didn't want to be stuck at home where he could watch that awful video over and over until he drove himself mad.

Instead, he caught a bus, then another, and another. He rode around thinking until he eventually wound up on the thirty three headed back toward the Sunder Estates.

He pulls his phone from his pocket, flicks on the torch, holds it aloft. The light is meagre, and cuts only a thin path through the gloom, but it's enough to give a little solidity to the wooden walls, the heavy door.

It looks uninviting. Maybe he should just go? There'd be no shame in that, he thinks. Yet he moves anyway, around the perimeter of the fence toward the gate.

It's an effort to squeeze through the gap on his own, but he does. When he steps up onto the deck, he raises a fist as if to knock at the cabin door, but he catches himself, lowers his hand slowly.

He has the feeling again that he's not alone. A sense that someone is on the other side of the door, waiting, watching.

The night is quiet. He has to listen hard to pick up the swish of canola plants in the breeze, a few insects buzzing, the soft drone of traffic far away.

He shakes off the jitters. Forces them down so his conscious brain can take control. He places a hand on the door handle, turns and pushes.

The cabin is dark. He raises his phone, shines it inside, first right to reveal the old bed frame and the kitchenette, then left where he finds the recliner, the odd television with the tumorous electronics. He realises he's holding his breath, exhales.

His first step inside feels awkward, heavy. It's like he's wading through something thick, viscous. Not night air, but oil. The second step is a little easier. As is the third.

He runs a hand along the arm of the recliner. The material is softer than he remembers. Well worn, but in a way that is comforting. It reminds him of his grandmother's house growing up, of the velvet bedspread in the spare room that covered the bed he'd stay in when he visited. He eases himself into the chair. The material caresses his back, his neck.

The television screen illuminates. A blue glow that grows steadily brighter.

His heart jumps in his chest, his muscles tense. His instincts tell him this is all too weird. They tell him to get up, run, but he doesn't. Because why else did he come here tonight? If not for this, then what?

The image on the television clarifies into that of the man that resembles Adrian very closely. The man he saw the other day. He's wearing glasses, has a little more grey at the temples than Adrian, and his neck is thickset, jowly. But otherwise, they could be twins.

The camera is jammed in tight on his face. It nearly fills the screen, but Adrian senses a hint of something odd behind him. The image is grainy, so it's hard to make out clearly, but it looks like flesh. Mounds of it, expanding and contracting like the body of a large, panting animal.

The man's voice—Other Adrian's voice —draws his attention. "Good," he says. "You're alone." His voice is gruffer than Adrian's, and his words are clipped. This is a man who has little time to waste on idle conversation and slow-witted people. Adrian swallows. He's not really sure what to say or what to ask. The words that spill from his mouth surprise him. "How did you get the video of my wife?"

Other Adrian frowns. Perhaps he expected Adrian to ask the who's, the what's, the why's.

"You are the three thousand, four hundred and twenty-third viable variant we have identified. But my agent tells me you are unusual. You do not possess a strong understanding of physics and mathematics."

It isn't phrased as a question, so Adrian doesn't answer. Odd words from the non-question ring loud in his head like the reverberation from a gong. Viable variant? Agent? He licks dry lips.

"I don't... don't understand what my education has to do with Candice?"

Other Adrian stares—a cold gaze. It is a foreign expression conveyed through Adrian's own eyes.

"Nevertheless, she indicated you have sufficient skills to build the receiver," he continues as if Adrian had not spoken. "How is your work progressing?"

"I haven't started," Adrian lies.

He sees a smirk at the corner of Other Adrian's lips. His image disappears from the screen, and is replaced with a shot of Adrian's open garage. From inside there comes a bright, pulsating light, the hiss and spit of the welder, the outline of Adrian in his protective coveralls, his welding helmet.

Adrian suspects the person who took this video is the same that took the video of Candice, and the hut. The agent. He glances toward the open door of the cabin as if he might find this agent standing there filming him now, but there's no one there. When he turns back, Other Adrian is on screen again, glaring, as if he is the one that has been slighted, not Adrian who is being tailed, filmed, shown videos of his wife.

"If you already knew, why even ask?" Adrian spits, angry.

His other self grins. An ugly expression that makes Adrian wonder what he looks like when he feels superior. Does he let it show like this man?

"I know what you're feeling. Or close enough. You're feeling lost, devoid of drive, stuck halfway between a decision made, and a decision to make. You're feeling like there's something more to all of this that you're missing. Something important. I'm here to tell you that there is. I can offer it to you."

Adrian licks his lips. Sweat beads on his forehead. "What are you offering exactly?"

"Knowledge and purpose. I'm offering a fractured piece of the picture its rightful place in the jigsaw puzzle. But this is conditional on you building that machine."

"The machine from your book," Adrian says.

"No, not my book. Another Adrian."

"Another?"

"There are as many versions of us as you can imagine. Some, like me, have made it our life's work to track them down."

"Why?"

A snort of laughter. "It's easier to show you, but I sense you are a stubborn one." He sighs. "Do you understand that in a single string of DNA lies all of the code to you? Everything you need to create a replica of yourself, Adrian?"

"I've heard something like that, yes."

"In the beginning, the universe was one. Then came the big bang. In that moment, everything changed. Not only was your universe formed, your stars, your planets, the seeds to human life on Earth, but so was my universe formed, and the universe of the man who wrote that book, and many, many more. The big bang did not just create, it divided. It split the singular into infinite realms. Only by drawing it all back together can we create the code, the DNA if you will, to what this all means."

"Life, the universe, and everything," Adrian says, smiling at his own joke.

Other Adrian frowns. Behind him, the flesh shudders.

"Mock if you wish, but we've already discovered much."

"We?"

"Of the viable variants I have located, six hundred and ninety-four have already joined me here, adding their knowledge to mine. This has given us some staggering insights. Our findings have been shared in my world, and developed into new medicines and treatments, which have allowed us to lengthen natural human lives. In my world, the average person is expected to live well beyond two hundred years."

"Two hundred," Adrian repeats, eyes wide. That seems ludicrous. And yet isn't talking to himself on a television ludicrous?

"That is just one of the discoveries we have made. A modest beginning. There is much more to do."

"But I don't understand how I can help you. You said it yourself, I have no knowledge of physics and mathematics," he says, a hint of sarcasm in his tone.

"Every Adrian is unique. Your experiences will help build our collective knowledge. I can show you how special you are."

Adrian licks his lips, processing. "All I have to do is build the machine?"

Other Adrian nods, tight lipped. Adrian senses something not said. That there is more to it than just a machine. But he doesn't probe.

"And what if I don't want to go further?

Other Adrian sighs. "I can only make an offer. It is up to you whether to accept or not. But I would ask you this: While you think about what I have said, continue to build. When you are done, return with your questions. If you are satisfied with my answers, then we will use your machine to bring you across to my world."

"And if I'm not, I stay here?"

The man gives a curt nod.

Ordinarily, Adrian doesn't think he'd be tempted by such uncertainty. But one thing Other Adrian says is right. He feels lost, stuck between places. And that video of Candice has set him spinning.

"Okay. I'll keep an open mind. I'll continue to build."

"Excellent. My agent will be in touch."

About four years after Adrian married Candice, he started to worry he'd run out of words. At least the meaningful words. He and Candice still talked about shopping lists, chores, how each other's day had been. They talked about renovations, and work colleagues. But none of that was real.

Then Candice surprised him with something that was.

Adrian had been asleep, early morning. It was Candice's perfume that woke him. He was somewhere in that place between light and dark, between dreams and reality, when her scent invaded—spring flowers, musk. Drowsy eyes opened and there she was, close, hair hanging half over her eyes. She was smiling when she kissed his neck, whispered: "What would you think if I stopped taking my pill?"

He swallowed hard, nearly choked on the saliva. Candice, thinking he was shocked, kept talking. "I mean we don't have to. I know we've never really... And things have been..."

Strained, he'd thought.

"Busy at work," she'd said. "But I guess I'm getting to that age and was thinking —"

"You read my mind," he interrupted, grinning. He rolled back so he could look at her more clearly. "Yes. I really want that. I don't know how to explain it, I just —"

"Want to bring something better into the world," Candice finished. He nodded. He felt tears welling, and he blinked rapidly to hold them back.

She made a strange noise in the back of her throat, leant close, kissed him. He apologised for his morning breath. She said she didn't care. They started trying that morning.

Candice told him it would take a few months to get the pill out of her system. Unfortunately, Candice's mother Alexia was diagnosed with cancer before that happened.

They kept trying intermittently, but without luck. And when they did, Adrian couldn't help but notice the change in Candice. The way she took control, rode him hard, aggressively, like she was angry, bitter. When he did ejaculate, which wasn't all the time, it felt weak and apologetic.

When Alexia died, they stopped having sex.

A month after the funeral, he found the new prescription in the medicine cabinet.

As Adrian finishes installing the battery in the machine, he hears Candice's car. He looks up to see it turn into the drive. He takes a deep breath, exhales loudly. He doesn't know what to feel around her at the moment.

The silence when she cuts the engine is deafening. The door groans as it opens, her high heels click on the cement. When she slams the door, it echoes around their suburban cul de-sac. Adrian flinches.

She walks toward him, and he feels himself shrinking, hoping she won't notice him at his bench. He turns and pretends to engross himself in his work. He hears the tenor of her footsteps change as she moves under the cover of the garage. Then she stops. He imagines her looking at the door to the house, then his back. The tension builds until he can't help but break it, like waves on a beach.

"Going out again?" he says. He hears the accusation in his voice, but hopes she doesn't. He doesn't want to start something.

"Yes. How are you going with the build?" He notices she doesn't invite him to join her. He wonders if she's visiting the man from the video. He doesn't even know how recent that was. She could have moved on. She may have multiple lovers. His hands are shaking. He lowers his tools, places them on the bench either side of the machine.

"It's going okay," he says.

"Do you know what it does? Or how it fits in with your game?"

He forgets sometimes that she still thinks he's solving a puzzle. But then again, isn't he?

"I'm not sure," he says, wondering how much he should say. He's been thinking about this a lot. He clears his throat. "I'm starting to wonder if it might be like a homing beacon. Something that identifies my location."

"Oh. So you turn it on, and if it works they know you've finished, and they come find you and give you a prize?"

His face contracts into a frown. Tension in his jaw, his cheeks. "Perhaps. Or they use my signal to contact me, and then they show me how to find them," he says, the thought concrete for the first time. He rises from his stool, steps back from the work bench, takes a couple of deep breaths and turns to face his wife.

She's looking away from him, back at her car. She's backlit by the afternoon sun, and strands of auburn hair drape across her right eye. In profile, she looks hauntingly beautiful. Adrian's heart jolts to see her. He wants to tell her everything.

She turns, smiles to find him looking at her. He feels connected to her in that moment. "Okay then. Well, I won't hold you up. I'm just going to change into some jeans and then I'll get out of your hair," she says, before moving again. He watches her walk toward the door, then she disappears inside. He wants to call after her, but can't. He wants to share his burden with her, but can't.

He follows her inside, hesitates by the kitchen. He can see the hall, but can't will his legs to move him there. He collapses more than sits at the kitchen bench, puts his head in his shaking hands, waits.

When she returns five minutes later, she doesn't really notice his state. She calls out a brusque farewell, and then is gone.

Before he hears her car start, his phone dings. He lifts his head from his hands. It feels heavy, like a bowling ball. His phone is where he left it, just by the box of tissues on the bench. It might be Candice, texting, "I love you". She does that sometimes.

But it's not. It's an email from an address he doesn't recognise. Redhead22@gmail.com. He normally wouldn't open it, but the subject line grabs his attention. "I can give you answers about the cabin."

He reads the email once, twice, then responds.

"Infinite Possibilities" continues in next month's issue.
See parts I and II of Michael Gardner's story "Infinite Possibilities" online at Metaphorosis.
If you liked it, leave a comment. Authors love that!
Remember to subscribe to our e-mail updates so you'll know when new stories are posted.

Copyright

Title information

Metaphorosis October 2022

ISSN: 2573-136X (online)
ISBN: 978-1-64076-238-1 (e-book)
ISBN: 978-1-64076-239-8 (paperback)

Copyright

Authors also retain copyrights to all other material in the anthology.

Works of fiction

This book contains works of fiction. Characters, dialogue, places, organizations, incidents, and events portrayed in the works are fictional and are products of the author's imagination or used fictitiously. Any resemblance to actual persons, places, organizations, or events is coincidental.

All rights reserved

Moral rights asserted

Each author whose work is included in this book has asserted their moral rights, including the right to be identified as the author of their respective work(s).

Publisher

Metaphorosis Magazine is an imprint of
Metaphorosis Publishing
Neskowin, OR, USA

www.metaphorosis.com

"Metaphorosis" is a registered trademark.

Discounts available

Substantial discounts are available for educational institutions, including writing workshops. Discounts are also available for quantity purchases. For details, contact Metaphorosis at metaphorosis.com/about

Metaphorosis Publishing

Metaphorosis offers beautifully written science fiction and fantasy. Our imprints include:

Metaphorosis Magazine
Plant Based Press
Verdage
Vestige

You can also find us:
@MetaphorosisMag, @Metaphorosis
www.facebook.com/metaphorosis

Help keep Metaphorosis running by supporting us at
Patreon.com/metaphorosis

See more about some of our books on the following pages.

Metaphorosis Magazine

Metaphorosis
a magazine of speculative fiction

Metaphorosis is an online speculative fiction magazine dedicated to quality writing. We publish an original story every week, along with author bios, interviews, and notes on story origins.

We also publish monthly print and e-book issues, as well as yearly Best of and Complete anthologies.

Come and see us online at magazine.Metaphorosis.com.

Plant Based Press

Vegan-friendly science fiction and fantasy, including anthologies of the year's best SFF stories, from 2016-2020.

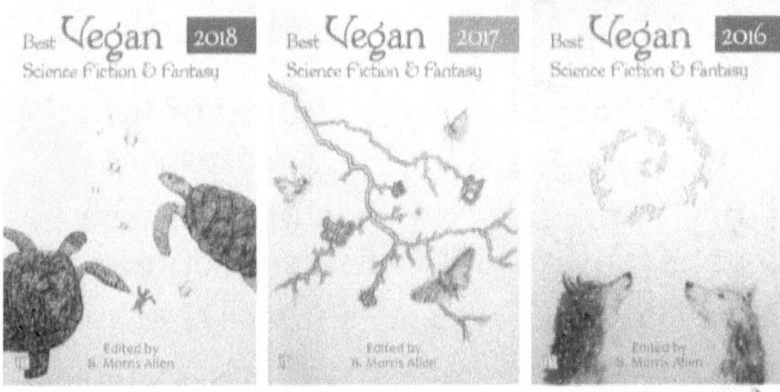

Chambers of the Heart

speculative stories
by
B. Morris Allen

A heart that's a building, a dog that's a program, a woman sinking irretrievably — stories about love, loss, and movement.

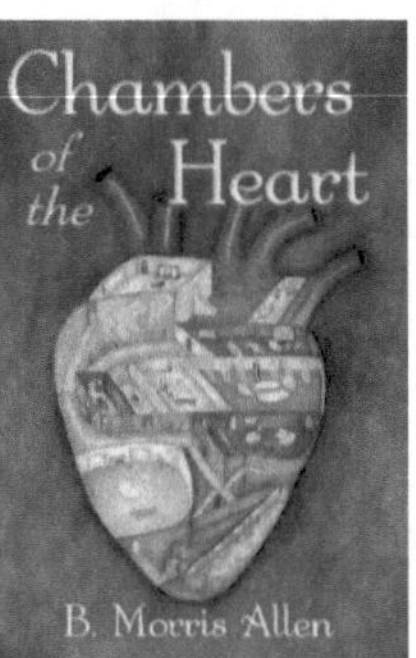

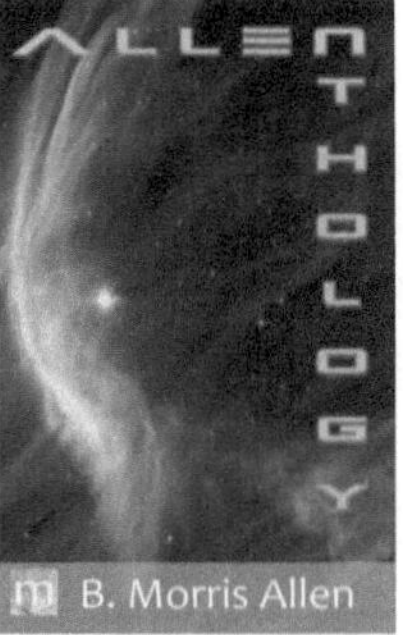

Susurrus

A darkly romantic story of magic, love, and suffering.

Allenthology: Volume I

Including three full collections of SFF stories.

Verdage

Science fiction and fantasy books for writers — full of great stories, often with an additional focus on the craft of speculative fiction writing.

Reading 5X5 x3

Changes

How do stories move from 'maybe' to published?

Here are 15 case studies of stories published in *Metaphorosis* magazine.

Reading 5X5 x2

Duets

How do authors' voices change when they collaborate?

A round-robin of five talented science fiction and fantasy authors collaborating with each other and writing solo.

Including stories by Evan Marcroft, David Gallay, J. Tynan Burke, L'Erin Ogle, and Douglas Anstruther.

Score

an SFF symphony

An anthology with an emotional score from the heights of joy to the depths of despair – but always with a little hope shining through.

Reading 5X5

Five stories, five times

See how different writers take on the same material.

Reading 5X5

Writers' Edition

Two extra stories, the story seed, and authors' notes on writing.

Vestige

Novelettes, novellas, and novels by Metaphorosis authors.

The Nocturnals
Mariah Montoya

Night is Dangerous. Day is deadly.

Where day and night last thirty years, humans move constantly stay ahead of the night and cruel Nocturnals that call it home. But a boy is lost out there.